THE APPLE OF HIS EYE

THE APPLE
OF HIS EYE

CATHY NISKA

iUniverse, Inc.
Bloomington

The Apple of His Eye

This is a work of fiction. All of the characters, names, incidents, organizations, and dialogue in this novel are either the products of the author's imagination or are used fictitiously.

iUniverse books may be ordered through booksellers or by contacting:

iUniverse
1663 Liberty Drive
Bloomington, IN 47403
www.iuniverse.com
1-800-Authors (1-800-288-4677)

Because of the dynamic nature of the Internet, any web addresses or links contained in this book may have changed since publication and may no longer be valid. The views expressed in this work are solely those of the author and do not necessarily reflect the views of the publisher, and the publisher hereby disclaims any responsibility for them.

Any people depicted in stock imagery provided by Thinkstock are models, and such images are being used for illustrative purposes only.
Certain stock imagery © Thinkstock.

ISBN: 978-1-4620-5287-5 (sc)
ISBN: 978-1-4620-5288-2 (hc)
ISBN: 978-1-4620-5289-9 (ebk)

Library of Congress Control Number: 2011916337

Printed in the United States of America

iUniverse rev. date: 09/08/2011

Dedicated to Joe for giving me the inspiration to follow through on my dreams, as you followed yours.

PROLOGUE

Every inch of the house was on fire, and when the last of the fire went out, there would be nothing left but a pile of ashes and dust. Tears dripped down Lissa Manelli's face as she watched the house come crashing down, bit by bit. A boy held her from behind, saying, "I'm so sorry, so sorry." He wished there was something, anything he could do for her, but he knew nothing could erase the pain she felt.

Lissa didn't move. She felt paralyzed, numb all over.

She prayed no one was inside, no one hurt or dead. She was only thirteen years old, and she had never seen a fire of this magnitude before. Had it been an accident or deliberately set? Whose house was it, and why did she have an intense fear that she was about to lose something precious because of it?

The boy behind her tightened his grip, offering her words of assurance. *Who was he?* she wondered. Her mind was drawing a blank. She could not figure out for the life of her who the boy was. She could not see his face, as if it were hidden by a thick fog in the starless night.

She shivered at not knowing who was with her and worried that something was wrong with her. Did it matter? Yes, it did.

She did not know what came over her, but in a flash she started running toward the house. She didn't know what she expected to accomplish. Run into the burning house, save whoever was inside, and risk her life in the process? She managed to run a few feet and then couldn't move an inch farther. The boy had grabbed her.

"No, you can't go, you have to stay here. It's too dangerous." The faceless boy tightened his grip even more.

Lissa wasn't thinking straight. She had the feeling of being in another world, another body. Nothing about this felt real. She was dreaming, had to be dreaming. All she had to do was wake up and everything would be right again.

A firefighter was talking to them, but she could not understand a word he said. "Blah blah blah," was all she heard, like when Charlie Brown's teacher spoke to him, never saying anything coherent.

Pop. She blew a bubble with the gum she was vigorously chomping on. Her tears fell more heavily as the house exploded, blown to bits and pieces. Everything in it would have been destroyed beyond recognition. Volunteers and firefighters ran in every direction away from the house. She spat the gum on the ground. It was tasteless after being chewed on for so long. Her jaw was starting to throb.

Wake up, Leigh.

Wake up, Lissa.

She was alone now; her companion had vanished. She felt his absence, felt so alone. She had never felt so alone in her whole life. Even though she had not known who he was, she missed his presence, yearned for him desperately.

She had to wake up before it was too late.

Time had passed. It was now seven years later, but she was still standing in front of the burning house. Her stomach bulged, testament to her late-term pregnancy. She smiled at her swollen belly, but no sooner did she do that than the bulge started to shrink, like the air leaking from a balloon. Here one second, gone the next.

She gulped hard. It hurt to swallow. Her throat throbbed, sandpaper rough.

"Ana Lissa!" Someone called to her, his or her voice echoing, sounding tinny. "You have to wake up. There isn't much time."

She knew that voice. Only one person had called her that in her life. It was . . .

She screamed, abruptly waking from the horrific nightmare, lungs on fire, sweat pouring off her. She had the feeling she had been bathed in sweat her whole nightmare. She took a few deep breaths, hoping to steady her heartbeat. Her heart was racing a million miles a minute.

"It was all a dream, all a dream," she told herself, sitting up while rubbing her arms, to get rid of the chill she felt.

Instinctively she knew part of the dream had been a reality once upon a time. "Who was in the house?" she wondered aloud. She hadn't a clue.

"My baby!" Lissa yelled, looking down at her stomach. She had a bad omen that she had just woken up from her second nightmare in less than a minute. Her previously bulging stomach had shrunk.

Her scream echoed across the city of Vancouver, British Columbia.

She had to be having the worst nightmares ever. When would she wake up? She had gone to bed pregnant and woken up seemingly not pregnant. What had happened while she was asleep?

She couldn't lift her arms. They were heavy, as though they were tied down with weights.

Bounding from bed, she could distinctly hear the sound of a baby crying. She knew it was hers. "Mommy's coming," she promised as she felt her way through the dark house, not having the energy to find a light switch. The crying grew farther away the closer she thought she was getting to her baby. Just as she thought she had reached him, could feel him, she collapsed and her world went black.

CHAPTER ONE

Christian Lynley smiled down at Lissa while she lay comatose in the hospital bed. Oh, how he loved her with every piece of his heart, his soul. The most beautiful woman in the world, she could have had any boy in school she desired. Most of the boys had vied for her attention, begging her to go out with them, so they could steal her heart. But her heart had already belonged to one boy and one boy only. She had only wanted one boy and had chosen—

"Christian!" Dr. Gabe Lucas's loud voice roused him from his daydream. "Earth to Christian."

"Sorry." He blushed as he came back to reality. "What did you find?" He was anxious to know what the test results had revealed.

Gabe hesitated, wondering how much to tell him. He knew that Christian and Lissa were associated somehow, but wasn't sure how. He had his theories, though. Lissa hadn't said much about the father of her baby. He couldn't put his finger on why it bothered him that she was so secretive about her past. It was almost as though she had something to hide.

Christian noticed the puzzled expression on Gabe's face and began worrying more. She was forty weeks pregnant and her due date was today. He had done the math months ago.

1

"She's not pregnant," Gabe said while glancing down at Lissa's motionless body. He wondered what had happened to her. She was alive, breathing, and stable, but she had been unconscious for hours, and he was worried.

She was his number one nurse, and he had hired her for the Director of Care position at the hospital's nursing home. She had done a remarkable job in the six months she had been there. After she finished medical school in a few years, she would be his number one doctor.

"What are you saying, Gabe?" Christian asked.

"Have you heard of phantom pregnancy?" He had had a phantom pregnancy case the day before. The strange part of that one was that that the father—or supposedly the father—had warned Gabe not to tell the woman that she wasn't pregnant. He asked Gabe just to tell her that she was experiencing Braxton Hicks contractions and to come back when her water broke. Though he wondered what he was going to do when the woman failed to produce a baby, he shrugged it off. Not his problem.

"Yes, I've heard of phantom pregnancies," Christian answered, "but Leigh was pregnant."

Christian calling Lissa "Leigh" startled Gabe at first, and then he remembered that for some reason, Christian always called her that. "The ultrasound shows no baby," Gabe said. "When I pushed on her abdomen, there was no placenta."

"There is a baby." Christian was adamant. Had Leigh given birth on the streets of downtown Vancouver, and their baby was lying somewhere on the streets, alone and abandoned, though through no fault of his mother's? Had someone picked him up and walked away with him? Had he been . . . ? Oh God. Grief consumed him. He would have to go back to where he had found her hours before.

Gabe hadn't wanted to broach his theory to Christian. Like Lissa, Christian was an excellent nurse and on his way to becoming an excellent doctor in the field of psychiatry. He and Lissa were like two peas in a pod.

"She was pregnant," Christian said. "I know for a fact she was, Gabe."

"So, you're the father." It was more a statement than a question.

"Yes, that is correct," Christian said. "So where's my son?" What had happened to the baby, his son, their son? He was determined to find him. He would find him.

Lissa slowly opened her eyes and tried to focus. The incessant beeps inside her brain were giving her a migraine. What were they? Why did they sound so familiar? Her vision blurry, she glanced around, noted the white walls, machinery, shabby furniture, and curtains that she had seen countless times before.

She was in the hospital. The realization jolted her. She lifted her hands and noticed the IV. What the hell? She tried to think back, remember, but her brain was like a blackboard erased of its previous contents.

She couldn't keep her eyes open. They became heavy again and closed against her will.

"My baby!" Lissa screamed.

Gabe had been reviewing her chart, and he rushed to her side. Tall, dark, and handsome, Gabe looked just like a prince. He was in his early forties, divorced ten years with no children. He was chief of staff at the hospital, and his employees and patients respected, trusted, and loved him. All he lacked was the perfect woman. He often thought she was just around the corner.

"Lissa, Lissa, wake up," he called to her gently. He didn't want to scare her; not knowing what had happened to her before Christian brought her in.

She placed a hand on her slightly rounded belly. He saw her glance at the ultrasound machine next to her bed, her expression confused.

"Stay calm," he said. He didn't want her to stress herself any more than she already was. They didn't know what they were dealing with yet. "Do you remember what happened?" he asked her.

She stared blankly at him. "What happened to me?" She was dumbfounded. She didn't have a clue what was going on, let alone what had happened. The migraine was still brewing, and not knowing what this man was talking about was worsening it.

She fidgeted with her hands, staring up at the man. She didn't have a clue what to say to him. "Who are you?" she asked.

"You don't know me?" He was obviously shocked.

"No." She shook her head. "Should I?" She continued staring at him.

"Do you know your name?"

"My name?" What had happened to her? She was not a Jane Doe, considering he had called her Lissa.

The door opened and a blond-haired man entered the room. He was no ugly duckling, but he was no prince from *Sleeping Beauty* either. It was obvious from his very worried expression that he had heard what she had said. He and the dark-haired man exchanged looks.

"Do you know me?" the second man asked as he approached her bed.

"Do you know me?" she asked instead. Staring at him, she wondered if she did know him and how. She could not keep her eyes off him; something about him pulled at her. Who was he to her?

Typical Lissa, Christian thought. Ask a question in order to avoid answering someone else's question, especially when she felt put on the spot. She tended to do that when she wanted to avoid the subject at hand.

"Why don't you answer me first?" he said.

"No, I don't know you. I don't know either of you."

Christian felt the blood drain from his face for the second time in the past few long and debilitating hours.

Oh, Christ. What now?

CHAPTER TWO

"I want to see my daughter," the man at the nurse's station demanded, a hint of authority in his voice. "Where the hell is my daughter?"

Phillip Manelli was under the impression that he owned the world and everyone in it. When he snapped his fingers, he expected the world to be handed to him on a gold platter.

"Where the hell is my daughter?" He smashed his fist on the counter of the nurse's station to emphasize his demand.

Phillip acted as though everyone was his friend. Actually, most people he knew were his enemies, but he called them friends. A hotheaded tycoon, Phillip was as ruthless as they came, and then some. A multibillionaire, he owned and managed dozens of businesses all over the world.

He had four loves, and they were (in order): his daughter, money, women, and his wife. He loved his wife more than life itself. She was the love of his life, and he couldn't and wouldn't live without her. She was just at the low end of the totem pole. He paid no mind to anything else, including his son.

"Sir, calm down, please," a nurse said, glancing up from her paperwork. "This is a hospital. People are sick and trying to sleep."

"You help me, I'll help you," he said, hoping she got his drift as he laid a hand on one of hers. "I want to see my daughter now," he said in a calmer tone. Still, his teeth were clenched, his free hand balled into a fist.

Christian approached, having overheard the conversation. "She's being examined by the doctors."

"Why are you still here?" Phillip asked. He didn't want this man anywhere near his daughter or grandchild, and he thought he had already made that abundantly clear.

It had been good of Christian to call him and tell him his daughter was in the hospital, but he'd told Christian not to be there when he arrived. He obviously needed to say it again.

"You know why I'm here," Christian said, "and I'm not going anywhere." Phillip didn't intimidate him, no matter how much he threw around his weight and power. It wouldn't work with him.

Phillip's phone rang. "What is it?" he said into the receiver as he walked away. "What do you mean? You had simple instructions. They weren't hard to follow." *If you want something done right the first time, do it yourself.* He cursed himself for not listening to his instincts.

He listened to the caller for a few seconds before saying, "Where is he now? You what?" He snapped the phone shut and went to sit down in the waiting room. This could not be happening.

Christian couldn't resist following him and asking, "Business deal gone wrong?"

"Shut up. Shut the hell up," Phillip said. "And get that smirk off your face." He sat silent for a few seconds, and then said, "You won't be here long."

"We'll just see about that," Christian said, crossing his arms over his chest. "I won't leave unless Leigh tells me to." Little chance of that happening unless her memory returned. That was assuming she wasn't faking having amnesia.

"How is she?" Phillip finally asked.

Christian rubbed his hands over his face, debating what to tell her father. "It's not good."

"What do you mean?" Phillip asked, panic in his voice.

"She appears to have amnesia." No point in delaying the inevitable. Phillip would find out anyway. "Or so it seems. And we don't know where the baby is."

Phillip's face twisted in a distorted way, so that he resembled someone having a stroke. He literally turned green, as if he was about to vomit. Christian turned and walked down the hall, asking a nurse to give Mr. Manelli some antacids.

"What is it about that kid I just don't like?" Phillip muttered after Christian left.

Obviously, Christian had known about the baby. He hadn't been sure before. His daughter had never said if she'd told him or not, but she didn't always say a lot when it came to the affairs of her heart.

Phillip thought about it, but couldn't quite put his finger on why he didn't like Christian. Hell, he'd known the kid since he was a young lad, but he'd grown up to be someone Phillip couldn't stand, and he didn't understand why his daughter or anyone gave him the time of day. It was his attitude, Phillip decided. His know-it-all, you-can't-touch-me attitude.

He'd talk to his daughter, make her listen to reason. Christian was no good. One way or another, he'd get him out of her life again, for good this time.

Gabe studied Lissa while checking her vitals. Her pale blonde hair shone in the sunlight. She was young and brilliant, ambitious, and smart, with a bright future in medicine ahead of her. This woman would go places other women could only dream about.

He had liked her so much when he met her six months ago, he'd hired her on the spot. He wished all his nurses and doctors were like her. When she smiled or laughed, she really lit up the room.

She'd been upfront with him from the beginning: that she was three months pregnant and wanted both to continue her studies and work through her pregnancy.

Gabe had frantically searched for a few months for another smart and ambitious nurse who could work with her at the nursing home. He had finally found Christian.

Out in the hall, Christian paced the floor, threatening to put holes in the already worn linoleum. He told himself it was better than holding up the walls. At least he was moving.

Christian had navy blue eyes and dirty blond hair. He was only about five nine in height, but had massive muscles bulging out everywhere, so that he resembled a bodybuilder.

He knew he wasn't the most gorgeous man on the block, but he wasn't ugly either. He considered himself average looking. He cared about those who touched his life. When he loved, he loved with his whole heart and would do anything for anyone he cared about.

The door to Lissa's room opened, and Gabe walked out. He and Christian walked down the hall, so they could talk in private.

"I don't understand what is going on," Gabe said, "other than the fact that she appears to have amnesia; she was pregnant and now she's not; and we don't know what happened to the baby." *If there was indeed a baby,* he added silently. Gabe was grief stricken, hoping her memory loss was temporary, and that she would start to remember when it was imperative for her to do so.

Pete Lynley caressed Lissa's face and then ran his fingers through her long, silky hair. She was asleep again, or pretending to be. He didn't care. He just wanted to be with her. He would be with her, her and their baby. He was kissing her face when the door unexpectedly opened.

"Who are you?" a doctor asked, storming into the room.

"I'm Lissa's fiancé," Pete said. "Where's the baby? Where's our baby? I can't wait to see him or her." He was ecstatic. He was a father, and the baby's mother was the love of his life. Maybe the baby was in the nursery.

Interesting, Gabe thought, staring at the man who looked oddly familiar. Two fathers. The first one—Christian—said son; this one was saying son or daughter. There could only be one father. If this man was telling the truth, what was Christian's story, and did he have anything to do with the missing baby? Christian had medical training, and he was the one who had found Lissa and brought her in.

He prayed Lissa got her memory back soon. Maybe there was more to Lissa, Christian, and this man than met the eye.

As Pete left the room, heading for the nursery, he ran into a man he hadn't expected, although he should have.

"What are you doing here?" Phillip asked harshly.

"I came to see my fiancée and baby," Pete told him. "I saw Lissa. Do you have any idea where our baby is?"

"In your dreams, Petey boy."

"Like hell!" Returning to Lissa's room, Christian had overheard the conversation and stalked over to the two men. He wanted to throw Pete out a window. For that matter, he wanted to throw both men out the window. He could take them both on.

"Sorry, little brother," Pete said. "This is my territory now." Pete smirked, enjoying the rise he was getting from his brother. The boys were three years apart in age, and to say they didn't get along was an understatement.

Pete continued. "Lissa and I had a long heart to heart yesterday, and we decided that we are going to get married and raise our baby together." Pete wasn't the least bit upset that the news would crush his brother. "And we made mad, hot passionate love to consummate our new union."

"Like hell," Christian said again. "You know you aren't the father."

Pete was hard pressed not to laugh. He and Lissa would just have to prove to his steroid-driven brother that Pete was the father.

"Get out now," Christian said, "before I rip you to shreds." His eyes were dark and threatening.

"How about the two of you get out now before I rip you both to shreds?" Phillip said. "Pete, the baby is missing, or at least we don't know where he or she is." Phillip was taking the initiative to inform father number two, since obviously Christian wasn't going to tell his brother.

Phillip honestly didn't know which one of them was the father, and secretively hoped neither one of them was. He had a distinct feeling he knew who the father was, regardless of whether it dismayed him or not. No one was good enough for his little girl, the apple of his eye. Was there a third contender?

Meanwhile, Pete's face had turned white as a ghost. "You mean, kidnapped?" he asked in horror.

CHAPTER THREE

So beautiful, just like your mother. Phillip smiled at his daughter as he entered her room. He had spoken to Dr. Gabe Lucas about Lissa's condition. Surely his daughter would know him, know who he was.

His daughter, his only daughter, *the apple of his eye.* Everything he'd done for her had been out of undying love for her, and he would continue protecting her, doing right by her until his last breath.

He would have paid her mortgage, bought her a new car, everything and anything she wanted in life, if she'd allowed him. Nevertheless, she hadn't. She didn't want his handouts. She was an independent woman. "I'm on my own now," she'd told him when he had brought the subject up. "I don't want or need you buying my life away."

Treading carefully as the doctor had advised him, he walked to her bedside. She was staring at the ceiling, her eyes unwavering. He touched her shoulder.

"Lissa?" It was a question. *Idiot.* He knew who she was. He tensed. The million-dollar question was, did she know who he was? He deluded himself into believing she'd turn around and fall into his arms, shed her tears on his shoulder; and he'd kiss all her troubles away as he had when she was a little girl.

If he knew his daughter as well as he thought he did, then even with her amnesia, there would be one thing, one key thing, she would want at this moment. Could he deliver? He knew she knew about the mysterious disappearance of her baby from her womb.

It seemed like an eternity before she turned and focused on him. "I want my baby." Introductions weren't necessary. He knew who she was, she didn't know who he was, but she knew who he was to her. Dr. Lucas had told him that she'd been informed that her father was there and desperate to see her.

He smiled at her, trailing a hand through her hair. "I'm sure there's a reasonable explanation, and we'll find your baby, my grandchild."

Phillip didn't want to hint to his daughter that he believed her baby was dead, or that a childless couple unable to have a baby of their own had kidnapped hers. Somehow, they had gotten their hands on the baby and left her for dead. What had she been doing in that alley? Tremors raced through his body at the thought of it.

Christian had found her in an alley close to where homeless people congregated. She had been unconscious, who knew how long. How had she'd gotten there? How had Christian known she was there?

With or without her memory, his daughter would frantically search the world for her baby until the day she died. Personally, he felt it would be a waste of time. If the baby had been kidnapped, it was probably halfway across the world by now. Lissa should just write it off like a bad check and go on with her life, and without those worthless boys that were no good for her. She should focus on finishing her education. She was still so young; she had her whole life ahead of her. After she finished school, she could find a man worthy of her, a rich doctor, and then think about having a baby.

A devious smile crossed his face. Maybe her amnesia would be to his advantage after all.

Either way, amnesia or not, he wondered if she'd ever be the same again without her baby and without the love of her life. She'd lived without the love of her life for the past six months, since relocating to Vancouver.

She'd been doing just fine and would continue to do just fine without that man and her baby. He had patted himself on his back for a job well done after he'd instigated that first separation. He had said to her, "Your brother needs you close to him while he undergoes rehab for his drinking." It was just too bad that she'd gotten pregnant before he'd convinced her to come to Vancouver. Otherwise, the Lynley boys would be history by now.

She'd reluctantly agreed at the time that relocating to Vancouver was the best thing, at least for now. She'd stay close to Chad, in case he needed her. He didn't have anyone else to turn to in Vancouver. So off they had gone, and she had said good-bye to the love of her life, but not forever, only temporary. So she'd believed.

As far as Phillip was concerned, couples went on after losing a child, either through no fault of their own or otherwise, even if they never accepted their loss. He had witnessed it himself, oh so many years ago. His gaze focused again on his troubled daughter, and he wondered what was on her mind.

"What happened to me?" she asked.

"I don't know, but I intend to find out."

"So you're my father?"

"Yes, I'm your father."

Lissa stared at him. With a father, usually there was a mother, but hers appeared to be absent. She was a mother and her child appeared to be absent. "Where's my mother?"

Her father raked a hand through his hair. Silence filled the room.

"My mother?" She was pleading, needing to know.

"She's dead."

Lissa closed her eyes in pain. She was beginning to think having amnesia was a good thing. Since waking up, she had found out she had no memory, her baby was missing, and her mother was dead. What next?

She looked at her father again. "How did she die?"

Lissa was silent while Dr. Lucas examined her. She stared at the white walls, not knowing what to say. She played with her fingers, twisted the rings around and around, thinking of how her life since waking up from a coma seemed like a merry-go-round.

She could have played with her rings for five minutes; it could have been hours. Tears ran down her face, as she felt like she was going into hysterics. She wanted her baby. Where was he or she?

She wanted her life back, her memory back. After everything she'd heard, though, she wasn't sure if she should run screaming out of the hospital or stick it out.

Lissa sighed in dismay as she considered what she'd learned so far.

In the few hours since she'd awakened, she'd met Dr. Gabe Lucas, her boss and friend. He appeared to be a good doctor, caring. Then there was Christian Lynley, a man from her past. He always seemed to be around. She wasn't sure what role he played in her life and if she liked it. He had also said he was her baby's father.

Then there was her father. She wasn't sure what to make of him, all doting, caring, and smiling. What was he thinking? She'd also learned that her mother, the most important person in her life, was dead. Her father hadn't even told her how she'd died. She could have been the key to bringing her memory back.

Her father's phone had conveniently rung before he'd had the chance to answer her. Was he going to tell her the truth, or give her some half-ass line and hope she believed him?

So there were three important people. There had to be more, and she would probably meet them before long. She had to talk to all of them one on one, have them help her put the pieces of her life back together. Most important of all, she had to find her baby.

Had she had her baby on the street somewhere and left him or her? Had she been attacked? She'd heard Christian had found her in an alley. Was his finding her a coincidence? What had happened before that?

Had Christian kidnapped her baby? Was he holding him hostage somewhere? Why, why would he do that? Was there something else going on here?

Where was she going to start to look for her baby? She had to get out of the hospital first. What should she do? Go to the police station and beg for assistance. But what could she tell them when she didn't know who she was? "My baby was stolen from my body . . . Oh yeah, by the way, I don't remember any of it and I don't remember who I am."

After Dr. Lucas left, on impulse she got out of the bed, dressed quickly, and walked out into the hall. She felt dizzy and lightheaded, her world spun like a top. She shrugged it off and proceeded down the hall. She would take some Tylenol or Advil when she got home. She made her way to the elevator, hoping she wouldn't see anyone who would prevent her from leaving. She managed to make it to the street, where she ran into a man who had the most beautiful face she had ever seen. She stared at him, awestruck.

"Where do you think you're going?" he asked, looking at her suspiciously.

Where was she going? "I-I-I don't know," she stuttered, still staring at the man. He didn't have the same build as Christian, but they were the same height. He had some muscle, as though he'd just started working out.

Pete Lynley couldn't believe Lissa's demeanor. She usually wasn't this passive with him.

"Did you get released from the hospital?" he asked, staying a slight distance away. The woman's moods could change with lightning speed.

"I released myself."

Typical Lissa, he thought. *She did what she wanted, when she wanted.*

"Who are you?" she asked.

The man gaped, not believing his ears. She didn't know him. What did that mean? No one had said anything about amnesia. All he knew was that his baby was missing.

"Pete." He held out his hand for her to shake it; she didn't reciprocate. "I'm your lover, your fiancé, the father of your baby, *our baby.*" He hoped to drill home a point, make her realize he was her destiny; they were each other's destiny. Who knew what lies his dastardly brother had been feeding her.

Good God, Lissa thought. *Two fathers.* She felt like she was going to faint from shock.

CHAPTER FOUR

Pete and Lissa sat in his silver Honda Civic. She continued staring at him. She couldn't get over his beauty, a blond Prince Charming from a fairy tale. Her staring seemed to embarrass him, for his cheeks were reddening as if he'd been out in the sun too long. He placed a hand on hers.

She didn't move her hand away, but noticed how cold his hand was. Finally she broke the silence between them. "So, you're *daddy?*" She was trying to make sense of it. Christian has said he was *daddy*. It wasn't possible that both of them to be the father. Maybe she had been intimate with both men and she didn't know which one was the father.

"Someone else said he was my baby's father," she added, still staring. He intrigued her, but she couldn't put her finger on why.

As though he sensed what she was thinking, he said, "He's lying."

"Who's lying?"

"My brother." She frowned in confusion, and he explained. "Christian, he's my brother. It's an understatement to say we don't get along."

"Why not?" She figured all siblings got along. If they didn't, there had to be a good reason, or a misunderstanding somewhere along the way.

You. Pete didn't say it, but he wanted to. He'd explain everything to her in due time, but first things were first. He leaned close to kiss her, his hand still on hers.

She backed away, her expression making it clear that she was not ready for that yet. *She needed answers,* he thought, answers that she probably hoped he would give her. He released her hand and clasped his own in his lap. Both of them were oblivious to anything around them in the hospital parking lot.

"So," she began, "we were a couple and conceived a baby?"

"Uh . . ." he started, thinking of how he should continue. "Not exactly." It was the truth, sort of. "We made a baby together, yes. That I am adamant about. This is our baby that's gone mysteriously missing."

"Why are you sure the baby is yours? Because I don't sleep around?"

Pete didn't know how to answer her. He'd like to believe that was the truth, but he hadn't convinced himself that that was the truth, or at least all of the truth.

"Tell me what's what then," Lissa said. *No more beating around the bush,* she thought. She had a baby to find. Whether or not Pete was the father was irrelevant now. One thing she knew for sure was that it was her baby. She'd worry about who the father was later.

He turned the key in the ignition. The engine revved, spat, and then started, barely. He glanced in the rearview mirror, and it seemed to her that he saw someone or something.

"Where are we going?" she asked. She wanted to know before he put the car in gear and drove away.

"I don't know yet."

"Are you going to help look for my baby?" Until she had solid proof he was the father, she'd refrain from saying *our* baby. It was *her* baby, and she intended to find him or her, even if she had to go it alone.

"Go back to your place, figure this out," Pete suggested. "Call the police."

They didn't live together. That was interesting.

"Do you know where I live?"

"Yes, of course I do. Don't be ridiculous." With that, he put the car in gear and took off like a shot.

"Slow down!" she said, frightened. He was driving like a manic, worse than a police car chasing after a speeding car.

He let up on the gas somewhat.

"So are you going to tell me about our relationship," she asked, "or keep me in the dark?" The dark was where she had been since waking up. She might as well live in a cave.

"Well, we're in love."

"We are or were?" She thought that was a good question, putting him on the spot.

"We are," he said. "We are in love, have been for years."

"Then what stopped us from being a couple?"

"Your father, my brother."

"What do they have to do with us being together if we're so happy and in love?" It didn't make sense. Something didn't add up. "What are we, Romeo and Juliet, forbidden lovers?" Were they going to commit suicide at the end of this tragic love story?

"Nobody is good enough for daddy's little girl."

"And your brother?"

"He's in love with you." He smiled at her and traced a finger over her face. "Or at least he thinks he is. He's slightly off the wall."

His phone rang. Pete looked at the caller ID, grimaced, and then silenced the phone and placed it in his shirt pocket. "They aren't as important as us. I'll call back or they will."

The phone call had disrupted the moment, may as well have been an earthquake.

"Who was it?"

"My mother." It wasn't a convenient time to talk, even to his ever-adoring mother. She'd be thrilled with the first part of his news, but heartbroken about the second part.

"Oh, Pete, that's wonderful to hear after all these years," she would exclaim at first. And then, "Oh, Pete, that's just awful. What can I do to help?" There would be tears in her eyes, and she'd be in Vancouver in a flash to do whatever she could to help.

"And you didn't answer her call," Lissa said.

"She'll understand. I'll call her back later or she'll call me back. She probably figures I'm busy."

"Does she like me?"

"In so many words." It would be difficult to explain. He patted her hand in a friendly way. "We're getting close to your house."

Lissa looked around as he drove through the city toward her house. It appeared that she lived in a suburban neighborhood.

It was still eating at her like a growing tumor. She had to know more, deserved to know more of how it had all come about. She turned back to Pete. "How did your brother come to the conclusion that he's the father and not you, considering he knows we were—sorry, *are* in love and sort of in a relationship and have slept together more than once I gather?"

Maybe she needed to ask Christian the same question, and she would. She was positive she'd be seeing him again soon, just as she was positive she'd been pregnant and her baby had been stolen from her, probably from inside her. The kidnappers might as well have ripped out her heart in the process.

"We are engaged," Pete reminded her.

He pulled up in her driveway then. At least she figured it was her driveway, her house.

Neither of them opened their doors. Pete said, "I don't know why Christian thinks he's the father. Maybe he drugged and raped you, or you slept with him unknowingly, and when he found out you were pregnant, he came to the conclusion that the baby's his."

Rape? Christian didn't seem like the type. He hadn't seemed even slightly bizarre, as Pete had put it. There had to be something else either Pete didn't know or wasn't divulging.

"All I know," Pete went on, "is that this baby is mine, not his. He always tried to come between us, was always jealous of me because you wanted and loved me and not him. He insisted that you loved him and that the two of you were meant to be. You never said much about your feelings for him. I don't think you ever wanted him sexually, but maybe some way somehow, he got you into bed without your knowing, my knowing." *It was a possibility*, Pete thought. "Or maybe you knew consciously without knowing, or thought it was me."

He banged both his hands on the steering wheel in frustration. "Can we kiss and make up now?" He hoped she'd at least commit to that, so they could get on with things, find their baby, get married, and get on with their lives. Things wouldn't turn out this way when they had their next baby. He would make damn sure of that. He touched a hand to her crotch, forgetting that she had just given birth and probably wouldn't be able to make love for several weeks. Even if it were possible for her to make love, he couldn't fathom the thought of seeing all that blood. It made him cringe.

They stared at each other again, seeking the truth, trying to figure out what the other was thinking.

They got out of the car, walked around to the front, and just stood there in silence, continuing their staring match. Slowly, as if in a slow-motion movie, they crept closer to each other, still staring, not daring to take their eyes off the other. Finally, their mouths met. His arms went around her; hers stayed by her side, not sure if she should touch this man. *Poison*, was the word that came to her clouded mind.

The feel of his lips weren't hot and sweet, not by a long shot. Pete's lips were icy cold. Her first thought was that he was a vampire." That was impossible. Vampires were fictional. Could she possibly have been in a relationship and conceived a baby with this man out of love? Could she have been in love with a man who was so very cold? She shivered thinking of it, thinking she was at the North Pole.

He must be naturally cold. Poor circulation. If he had been honest with her from the start, if he was indeed telling the truth about her baby being their baby, and that they were destined to be together, they would work on his circulation problems together. After all, she was a nurse on her way to becoming a doctor. She knew about this stuff.

There was a bang on the hood of the car. Pete and Lissa jumped back from each other. Blushing, Lissa looked up into Christian's eyes. She had been right about seeing him soon.

"Get your hands off her." Christian's tone sounded threatening. The fire in his eyes made him look ready to kill. *Maybe he could send some of that fire to his brother,* Lissa thought, *heat him up.*

"Make me," Pete said. He tightened his grip around Lissa's waist.

No sooner had Pete pulled her closer, than his brother's fist landed on his Pete's eye. His grip loosened as he instinctively raised his hand to his injured eye.

The brothers stared at each other. One had ice in his eyes, the other fire. Knowing his brother, Pete wasn't going to give him the satisfaction of hitting him back. He did not want to make a spectacle in front of Lissa.

"I feel like I live in a soap opera," she said. "Are you sure we aren't in Salem, Genoa City, or Port Hope?" She started toward her house, leaving them glowering. She hoped they weren't going to kill each other.

CHAPTER FIVE

Lissa lived in an end-unit townhouse. The brick was a reddish brown. She had a double garage. There were six homes in the complex.

While fishing for her keys in her purse, she looked at her house. Did she own it, did she rent? Did she know her neighbors? Did they know her? Had her father bought her the house, or paid the rent?

Since she was pregnant, what kind of life had she led since moving to Vancouver? She'd been told she'd moved here from Briarton six months prior. Was she sociable, antisocial? Did she have many friends, few friends, or no friends?

Would she ever be able to remember who she was before? Before what? She wasn't sure how to react to those thoughts. She needed something, anything, to jog her memory, help her remember. She wished her mother were alive to help her through this, tell her what to do, tell her who she'd been involved with before. If it was possible that she'd slept with more than one man, and if those two men had been brothers.

Inside her house, she quickly surveyed her surroundings and located her cordless phone. She found the number for the police department and dialed. When the dispatcher answered, she said, "My baby was kidnapped under unusual circumstances."

The dispatcher asked questions and she relayed what she knew, which when she thought about it, wasn't much.

"I have to find my baby, my life depends on it." She imagined her statement wasn't unusual, coming from a mother whose child was missing. She'd heard that some women regained their memory after seeing their child. She hoped this would be the case, if she didn't start remembering soon. She was damned determined to find her baby, even if she died trying.

By the time the call ended, her body was trembling like a leaf in the wind. The dispatcher had told her that a police officer would be at her house as soon as possible.

An endless, anxious wait it would be. She decided to make some use of the time. She started in the garage, where she found a late-model maroon Honda CR-V and a slightly older silver Acura ZDX. Going through the glove compartments, she found the registrations, which confirmed she was the owner of both vehicles.

After the garage, she through the house, top to bottom. She found the master suite. Did she live here alone? A queen-size bed, wardrobe, two dressers in the master suite, an adjoining full bath. Three more bedrooms furnished with exuberant colors from pinks to blues, greens to reds, one with a queen bed, the other two with singles.

One small room was an office. On the desk was a desktop computer, printer, and phone. There were tons of notes on the desk. One in particular read, "call Lyn to talk about what's next, future." *Hmm, interesting.* Had she been referring to Christian or Pete? One of them was definitely the father of her baby, the note almost proved it, but which one? She hadn't been entirely convinced of Pete's story. There were holes in it bigger than a grave.

It made her wonder why Christian came to her defense, so to speak, to get Pete off her. Why had he done that? She really needed to talk to him in private.

Another room, obviously the nursery, was filled with a crib and a bassinet, a changing table, dresser, and a wardrobe. Baby clothes and toys were everywhere, and a mobile hung over the crib. Everything a nursery should have, and more. Had she done this herself? Everything in the room was unisex, so she figured she hadn't known the sex of the baby.

A wet feeling inside her pants warned her that it was time for a change of pad. Searching all three bathrooms in the house, she found she had no maxi pads or tampons. She checked the time. Not wanting to miss the police officer, she didn't dare run to the store to get sanitary products. Ask one of the boys? Fat chance.

She took a quick shower to get the slime and odor off her body. Afterwards, she changed into black yoga pants and a red sweatshirt. It was a little cool outside for April.

In the kitchen, she looked out the window at the backyard, with an in-ground pool, deck, and grill. The refrigerator was filled with food. She wouldn't go hungry or have to go grocery shopping for weeks.

The massive townhouse, with its oak flooring and expensive furniture, the full gym in the basement and the two cars in the garage, made her wonder who had paid for all this stuff. She had been told her father was a multibillionaire, but she also knew she had a good job with a handsome salary as well.

It made her feel weird to think her father might be paying for her lavish lifestyle.

Checking the time, she noticed she'd been inside for about half an hour, probably too long to leave the two goons outside alone. Still, it was their battle. She wasn't getting involved in it unless one or both of them forced her to intervene.

Peering out her living room window, she saw that they hadn't killed each other yet. If they did go at it, could she say, May the best man win? Looking more closely, she saw that they weren't alone. A third man wearing a dark uniform had arrived. Maybe he was the police officer.

She saw Christian hand a cell phone to Pete and he started talking. She could see his lips moving. Maybe it was their mother again. The call ended, and the three of them headed toward the front door. Oh, God!

Now Lissa was able to get a better look at the third man. Handsome devil. She wondered if they knew one another. Two Prince Charmings and one ordinary-looking guy. She knew she was beautiful. The mirror in her bathroom had told her that, and so had a few people at the hospital after she woke up. Would she have had a relationship with an average guy like Christian, when she probably had had endless choices of men? She supposed that depended on how she felt about him, before.

Taking her gaze off Christian and putting it on the police officer, she wondered again if they knew each other, had a past? Could he be contender number three in the mystery of *who's the daddy?* And could she have slept around that much? She was giving herself a bad rep.

The three men entered the house and came into the living room. Only one of them removed his shoes, Christian.

"Lissa, I'm Liam McCall." The police officer introduced himself and shook her hand.

"Do we know each other?" She had to ask, had to know.

"Yes, we met when you first came to Vancouver. We've been chummy ever since."

Chummy. What did that mean?

"I'm so sorry about your baby," he said.

Not our *baby?* she thought.

"The police force and Christian and I are going to do everything possible to find your baby." There it was again, *your* baby. She noted that he hadn't included Pete in the "find" part of the conversation.

"Where do we begin?" She was eager to get started, right now.

"Christian and I are going to work together with you to bring your baby home safe and sound." There was a positive tone to his voice, almost an exuberance. And *safe and sound* were such reassuring words. She had no doubts that he was trained to use those words.

"Since Christian is studying psychiatry," Liam went on, "he wants to work with you to help try to recover your memory."

Wow, he was the spokesperson for all three of them. Neither of the other two men had uttered a word since they came in the house. While Liam talked, the brothers stared intently at her. She wondered what they were thinking. She did note that Pete's face paled at the mention of Christian working with her to restore her memory. He also seemed surprised by some of the things Liam had said.

Pete was surprised. *Surely,* he thought, *his brother didn't have the kind of training yet to help Lissa., yet. School, what a waste of time when there were so many other important things to be doing.*

"So, Pete?" Liam asked. "Are you with us or on your own?"

Pete didn't like the was Liam was looking at him. It was obvious the police officer didn't like him. Feeling uncomfortable, Pete stuttered, "I-I think I'll work alone. I probably have a better chance of finding Lissa's and my baby on my own." It may have been his ego talking, saying he had a better chance.

That's because Pete knows where the baby is, Christian immediately thought. He was almost convinced Pete was part of the whole baby disappearing act. Instinct told him to have him followed. Maybe Drew would be up for the challenge. Drew was a longtime friend of his and Lissa's, and conveniently was also a PI.

"Well, don't let us keep you," Christian said, hoping his brother would take the hint.

Lissa had gone into the kitchen and come back with an ice pack for Pete's now swollen eye. She handed it to him and then sat down on the couch. She was exhausted and still feeling dizzy and light-headed. She'd forgotten about taking pain medication, but she didn't recall seeing any.

"Call when you find something," she said to Pete. "And be careful."

"I will. You'll be first to know, the first one I call." He smiled and walked over to her, intending to kiss her good-bye. The darts in his brother's eyes halted him. That would have to wait until later when they were alone, *very alone*. She'd come to him with her tail between her legs . . . No, that was him. But she'd come to him nonetheless, wanting him, begging him, screaming for him. *Pete*.

No one waved or said good-bye as he left.

After he was sure Pete was gone, Christian spoke. "You don't remember anything before waking up?"

"Nothing conclusive."

"What do you mean by 'conclusive'?" He liked to think he knew her well, better than anyone else did, but now he wasn't so sure. It was as though by losing her memory, she had changed somehow, become more guarded and jaded. He'd have to talk to her alone. "Come on, Leigh. Talk to me."

"Why do you call me Leigh?"

"That's what I call you. I haven't called you anything else in years."

"How many years?"

"About seven."

Lissa shook her head, as if annoyed with their sidetrack into their past. "This isn't helping to find my baby."

"Our son," Christian retorted. "And no, it isn't. We can rehash our past later." And they would. He was damned and determined.

"How do you know it's yours and how do you know it's a boy?"

Liam excused himself to call the station. He knew he didn't belong in this conversation.

"I was there when he was conceived," he answered Lissa. "Neither of us slept around with other people."

He knew that, just as he knew her baby was his baby, their baby. If something had changed since their breakup and there had been other men for her, that was a completely different ballgame. She had been pregnant when she had left their home in Briarton to come to Vancouver six months ago. He was one hundred percent certain of that.

"How do you know the baby's a boy?" Lissa asked, knowing she might not like the answer. "Is it because you kidnapped him and that's how you know? And now you're hiding him somewhere as some kind of payback for my leaving you?" She didn't have her memory, but she could derive a conclusion. She knew from her father that when she had left Briarton for Vancouver, she had left someone significant behind.

"I did not kidnap *our* son," he said, obviously upset by her harsh words. He stared at her, his eyes not wavering as he told her he had nothing to do with the kidnapping.

"Then who did?"

"I have my suspicions."

"And I have mine." She watched his eyes. She wanted to believe him, really wanted to believe him. Actually, a part of her did and a part of her didn't. How could he know it was a boy and not a girl, if he hadn't already seen the baby?

Liam walked back into the living room. "Christian, where have you been between last night and now?"

CHAPTER SIX

Christian coughed. "At the nursing home, working." He had been there from eleven the previous night until seven thirty that morning. After his shift ended he had gone jogging, and that's when he'd found Lissa.

He had planned on checking on her after going home and showering, to see if she'd had any signs of labor yet. Also, he wanted to talk to her, really talk to her. They needed to talk, still needed to talk, now more than ever. Her amnesia complicated things more than ever.

"And that can be verified?" Liam asked. He knew that Christian's time at the nursing home could be checked out. He could look at time sheets, talk to other staff that were on the previous night. But what had Christian been doing before and after work?

After overhearing part of Lissa and Christian's conversation, he also wondered how Christian knew the baby was a boy. That he'd ask him later. What he really needed was for Lissa to regain her memory. That would break the case wide open.

"After my shift was over," Christian said, "I went home, changed, and went running. That's when I found Leigh lying in that alley downtown. She was unconscious, and I brought her to the hospital."

That sounded logical to Liam.

"And the baby?" he asked.

"I didn't realize she'd already given birth."

"Who did you call on your way to the hospital?" Liam knew he'd made a call.

"Gabe. That is, Dr. Lucas, to tell him we were coming in, and that something was wrong."

"Why didn't you call me?" He'd wondered that all day. Christian hadn't called him. They were friends after all. Why? Was there something else? Was he hiding something?

"Like I said, I didn't know at first that she had already given birth."

"But after you found out that she had given birth and came to the conclusion that the baby had been kidnapped, you still didn't call me?"

"I didn't think at first that our son had been kidnapped. I thought maybe she'd asked someone to watch him."

"Wouldn't have she called you upon going into labor?"

"I would think so, but sometimes Leigh does things that surprise you." Like when she told him, she was pregnant in a roundabout way, without really telling him.

"You know, don't you?" she had asked him on the phone one night. He had just asked her if she was okay, if she needed anything.

"Yes, I know," he had replied.

"No, I don't need anything," she'd said. "I'm fine, I'm good."

He smiled shyly at both Liam and Leigh. "She e-mailed me all the ultrasounds."

Lissa thought about that. "Is that how you know the baby's a boy?" she asked.

Christian turned a pinkish red. "Yes, I peeked. I enlarged one on the computer and saw the male anatomy. I thought it was a boy, and I wanted to see if I was right."

Christian's story was pretty convincing, Lissa thought. So where did Pete fit into the equation? She was sure he had a role in this somewhere. By why were they talking about the past instead of going out there and searching for the baby? She didn't see how any of this was significant or would help find her kidnapped baby.

She wondered if the baby resembled more his mother or his father, or was a bit of both. Could he possibly be the spitting image of one of them?

"Are we going to stick around here and pick our asses, rehashing the irrelevant past?" she yelled. "Or are we going to go out and look for the baby?" Tears were threatening to fall.

"The past is the key." Christian said. "Your past is the key." He sat beside her and placed a hand on her shoulder. "Regaining your memory, remembering who you were, who we were and are to each other, it's all key information. Our son's kidnapping could go back as far as to when you were born." His classes in psychiatry had taught him a lot, how to read between the lines, and especially that the past was the key to everything.

Lissa felt instant heat when he laid a hand on her shoulder, like a heating pad. Was there any logic to what he was saying? Could he be onto something?

"How is the past going to help when I don't even remember who I was?" she asked.

"You do remember, it's locked inside your brain," he said. "We'll work together, help you regain your memory."

Would he? she wondered. *Would he really?*

"Do you want to stay here and talk to Liam for a while?" he asked. "Or do you want to come with me?"

"Where are you going?" Did she care? Yes, if it had something to do with the baby, yes, she cared. Like if Christian was going to go see him, check on him.

"Home," he answered. He hoped that he had enough schooling to do what he wanted to accomplish.

"I'll stay here," she said, thinking this was her chance to talk to Liam alone, in private.

Liam quashed that idea. "I have to go back to the station," he said. "I can come back later, if you want."

Liam left first. Christian stood in front of her for a few seconds, watching her carefully. "We'll find our son," he promised. He bent down and kissed her, barely touching his lips to hers, as if wanting to test her reaction.

As quickly as his lips were on hers, they were gone. *Wow,* she thought. What was that? He had barely touched her, but powerful currents ran through her body, as if she'd just experienced electrical shock. *Papa, come to Mama,* she thought.

He walked to the door and left, saying, "I love you, Leigh, and you have no idea how much."

She placed a single finger on her lips after he'd closed and locked the door. "I love you, Lyn." She heard herself speak, but didn't not know where the words had come from. She closed her eyes, just wanting to rest for a minute. In seconds, she was out cold.

Christian walked down her driveway, thinking they were no further ahead after what felt like hours of rehashing of the past and Liam's interrogation, than they had been when Leigh woke up with amnesia at the hospital earlier. He wasn't surprised to see that Liam was waiting for him.

"What's up, Liam?" Christian braced himself for more of his friend's interrogation. He knew Liam had to do it, it was his job. He didn't have to like it, though.

"Other than your brother," Liam said, "do you consider anyone else a suspect?"

Christian didn't have to think about it. Still, he hesitated for a moment before mumbling a name.

A few minutes later, both men drove off in opposite directions. They each had their own destinations, their own agendas.

He drove erratically, frantically searching for the place he was looking for. He'd already driven around too long for his liking. He'd find it. He'd be damned, but he'd find it. He consulted the map one last time and concluded that the place he was looking for was right around the corner.

Through the numerous trees in the woodsy area, he found the cabin he was looking for, right around the corner as the map had indicated. He smiled a devilish smile.

No car was in the driveway. It was probably in the garage. He bounded from the car, heard the roar of the ocean down below, and started toward the front door.

Locked, damn. The lights were on, so someone was there. She was there. He banged on the door and yelled. "Let me in. It's safe."

One minute, two minutes, three minutes, and she opened the door, holding a screaming baby.

"Idiot," he said. "You shouldn't have opened the door without asking who it was."

"I checked through the window," she said. "Besides, I knew it was you."

He walked into the cabin, shutting and locking the door behind him. "So you did take my baby."

Looking at the baby, even he couldn't deny who the father was.

"I didn't take anyone's baby. This is my baby," the young woman said, holding the baby closer to her, protecting it.

"So, you didn't take the baby from the van and run away with her while I dealt with her mother?" he asked, though he knew that she had.

"I am her mother," she said, She looked confused. "I gave birth to her this morning. I called you to tell you, but you didn't answer." She pouted, her lips protruding.

"I've been busy putting out fires," he explained, taking another peek at the baby she held. "Some of them you started."

The baby wailed long and hard.

"Meet our daughter, Lynley," she said. "Isn't she beautiful?"

"Our what?" The man named Lynley choked in shock. How was he going to get out of this one? He felt the walls tumbling down around him. "What are you talking about?" Something was definitely not right with this girl.

"What are we going to name her?" the girl asked excitedly. "What are we going to name our daughter?"

CHAPTER SEVEN

Shivers ran through her while Pete's hands caressed every inch of her body. Why did he have such a low body temperature? Was he just inhuman as she'd first thought? She imagined herself picking icicles off her body when they were through, or thawing herself in a steamy hot shower. Now, there was an idea. They could build heat together.

He kissed every inch of her body, as thorough as a dog that never misses a speck of food while licking his bowl clean.

When he slid his finger inside her, she had the illusion of a Popsicle inside her. He built her excitement, making her moan and groan. When they were both ready, he entered her. No need for protection. They already had a child and would likely have others.

As they moved together, pleasing each other, she had the image of his male anatomy being nothing more than an ice cube edged with frost inside her.

Lissa woke up shivering. Her teeth were chattering. Rising from the couch, she checked the thermostat. No wonder she was freezing. The air conditioner had been adjusted so high, the house couldn't get any colder. She adjusted the temperature, turning the heat on.

She also turned on the gas fireplace and grabbed the comforter off the back of the couch. She'd be toasty warm in no time. She lay back down, hoping she didn't have another dream like that.

Before dozing off again, she thought about the lovemaking between her and Pete in her dream. She didn't think she would ever be able to make love to a man, love a man, and conceive a baby with a man who was so cold. There was obviously something wrong with him. He needed to see a doctor. She'd mention it to him if she found him so cold next time she saw him.

Lissa and Liam pulled back from their kiss. It had been acceptable but not particularly exciting for either of them, especially when he touched her belly and felt the bump that was growing there.

"Huh?" He looked at her in surprise.

"Sorry." Her face warmed with a flush of embarrassment. "Sorry I didn't tell you," she continued sheepishly. "I'm not looking for a daddy for my baby. My baby has one, and he will be here by the time he or she is born."

"Oh." He didn't seem to know what else to say. "You know that for sure? Are you in love with him, the father of your baby?"

"Yes, he's the love of my life."

"I see."

She watched his face as he reassessed the possibilities of their relationship. They would not become a couple. But friends could kiss friends, and there was also friends with benefits. They puckered up their lips, drew closer to until their lips were within breathing distance of each other and—

The doorbell rang.

Lissa bolted up off the couch at the sound of the doorbell. "My baby is home! My baby!" She jumped for joy and almost ran to the door.

When she opened it, she found Liam leaning against the doorframe.

"You look a little flustered," he said. "Are you okay?" Concern rose in his voice.

"Weird dreams," she explained, brushing it off while motioning him in. "Any news?" She didn't want to dash her hopes, but she was optimistic that her baby would be home soon.

"No. Sorry to be the bearer of bad news. But on another note, no news is good news."

She wouldn't cry. She had to stay strong, stay optimistic, and think positive.

"How are you holding up?" Liam asked. He wanted to touch her, at least take her hand or even give her a friendly hug, but didn't out of fear he'd scare her. He had his own issues to deal with. They'd been through the emotions of a more-than-friends relationship in the past; and they'd decided that, baby or no baby, they were better off as just friends.

"As well as can be expected, I guess," Lissa answered. How was she supposed to be holding up? She had no memory, no recollection of her past. Everything was gone. All she knew was that someone had ripped her baby out of her and now he was missing.

"It's okay to cry," he said.

She wanted to, had to, but was bottling it all up inside. Eventually, she knew, it would burst free, and it would be hard. She just hoped that she wasn't alone when it happened, that she was with someone who understood and could help her through her grief.

But no, she contradicted herself. Not in front of Liam, not in front of anyone. She wouldn't subject anyone to that. It would be so unfair to the person on the receiving end, especially if he or she didn't understand or know what she was going through.

"I'm okay," she lied, turning away.

Again, Liam wanted to console her, hug her, he wasn't sure that was a good idea. He didn't know how she was feeling, and couldn't possibly imagine what she was going through. He wasn't sure if he'd ever be a father, and if he was, he hoped he never experienced this kind of pain.

"If you want to talk about it, I'm a good listener," he said. That was probably the best he could offer her now, unless he got a lead on her case. He hoped for her sake, the baby's sake, and the baby's father's sake they would get a break in the case soon.

He was surprised they hadn't received a ransom note. This worried him. It wasn't particularly good news for them.

His phone rang, and he scowled when he saw the name on the caller ID. He almost hit *decline*, but thought better of it. Still, he cringed when he answered the call.

"And how are things going?" the caller asked with ice in his voice.

"How do you think things are going?" he snapped. "This isn't working out as planned."

"Definitely not," the caller agreed. The additional complication had royally screwed things up. "How do you expect to fix this?"

"Why me?"

"Your screwup."

"I didn't expect this to happen," the first man said. "It was supposed to be easy as pie."

"Yes. But you screwed it up and now you're going to fix it. You're going to find that baby and bring him to me, so I can settle scores with its parents." He had a lot riding on this baby. His whole life, his future.

A smile flashed across the first man's face. He'd already gained an advantage over the caller, and now he was ahead of the game. He snapped the phone shut. They were playing by his rules now.

He was the one in charge and he'd come out on top. Before long he'd have the woman and the baby, and they'd move far away from here, to where they could be alone.

He didn't know how he was going to do it yet, but he would. He'd get the woman, the baby, and everything else he'd ever wanted in life, including the loot. Screw work, screw school. He'd be living the high life that he was meant to live.

His phone rang again. This time he hit *decline* and continued on his way.

Lissa debated asking Liam what their relationship had been and what, if anything, had happened between them, either romantically or otherwise. The sound of the doorbell halted her.

She rushed to the door in anticipation, but standing there was a woman about fifty years in age.

"Oh, Lissa you're home. Did you have the baby? Was it a boy or a girl? As I told you, a boy was my prediction. Can I see him? Is he awake? What did you call him?" The questions raced out of the woman's mouth at a mile a minute, one after the other without pause.

What could she tell the woman? She'd be able to tell from Lissa's size that she was no longer pregnant.

"Yes, I did have the baby." Lissa smiled, struggling to recall the woman's name.

"Was that last night? I saw a few cars here and there, coming and leaving and coming back again, cars I've never seen here before." She paused, seemed to sense Lissa reluctance to talk. "Oh, I'm so sorry. You just had a baby, you're probably stressed out. I can come back, or you can come by when you're not so busy. And bring the baby."

"What brings you by?" Lissa asked, trying to pretend everything was all right.

"Oh, I wanted some of that aloe lotion you make, but it can wait until later,"

Lissa struggled to remember again, pressing a hand to her forehead as though to ward off a headache. She recalled seeing some homemade remedies when she had first explored the house earlier that day. "If you write down which one you want, I'll get it to you later on."

Liam joined her at the door. "What cars did you see here last night and what time?" he asked the woman.

"Around eleven," the woman answered readily. "Well, shortly after eleven and then most of the night. A white van at least ten years old, and a fancy-dancy car like some rich guy would drive. It was dark, navy blue or black, and then there was a Sunfire."

"Why were you up so late?" Liam asked.

"Oh, my granddaughter was staying over. She fell ill, so my husband and I ran out a few times to get her some soup and medicine, and then take her home."

"When did you see the first car?" Liam asked.

"Lissa's light went out around eleven—that's when I went out to the grocery store—but her TV was still on. I came back about half an hour later, her TV was off and the white van was in her driveway then. My husband went out shortly after to pick up some medicine, and when he came home, he said the van was gone. About an hour later, the van was back, and a Sunfire was there too. When we took our granddaughter home an hour later, the van was there, the Sunfire was gone, and the fancy car was there. There were hardly any lights on at the time. That was about four in the morning."

Liam jotted down notes in his pad as the woman told her story.

"Then," she went on, "my husband got a snack attack, so he went out for some pizza. When he came home, he said no cars were here and all the lights were out, but he was positive he saw a someone standing in front of the front door. He couldn't tell who it was since it was so dark. He didn't want to be nosy and alarm the person, but he did think it was Lissa."

Liam stayed silent. He suspected Mrs. Nosy wasn't quite finished.

Sure enough, she continued. "When I went out around eight this morning, a Honda Civic was in the driveway, but it was gone when I came back." She glanced at Lissa. "This is a very busy house."

Liam gave Lissa a nudge to indicate that she should shuffle the woman along her way. "Yes, very busy indeed," Lissa said. "If you just write down what you want . . . Or I can look it up in your file if you want the same thing. I will bring it over little bit later on." To tell Mrs. Nosy that her baby had been kidnapped and she and her husband possibly were witnesses to that crime was not something Lissa was going to get into with her.

As Liam handed the woman a pen and paper, he wondered if Lissa was faking her amnesia. Maybe she remembered everything except the labor, birth, and kidnapping of her baby, which would be understandable. People sometimes forgot traumatic events.

The woman handed Lissa back the pen and paper and went on her way.

Liam's thoughts continued spinning as Lissa closed the door. Did she have something to do with her own baby's disappearance? The fancy car the woman had described sounded like one her father would drive, or a well-to-do doctor.

What was her game? What the hell was she up to? What did she expect to accomplish by faking her amnesia?

And where the hell was Christian? And Pete?

"Well now, what do we have here?" the man asked the young woman as he walked uninvited into her home. "Does your mother know you had a baby?"

"No." She moved away from him. She had always been terrified of this man.

"And don't you think you should tell her? I think she'd want to know, so she could lend her support, lend a hand. She's been looking for you for months. She's been worried."

The girl was speechless.

"Let me hold the baby." He gestured for her to give him the baby. She didn't move. "Bessie," he said, urging her.

She had an eerie and uneasy feeling. She didn't want to relinquish the crying baby to this man now or ever. She was deathly afraid of him, always had been.

Someone else walked into the room. The older man turned around and stared into the face of a younger man. He sneered. "You?"

"You?" The young man sneered right back at the older man.

"You?" Bessie stared at both men.

"Keep your hands away from my daughter and my girlfriend," the younger man demanded. He laid a protective arm around Bessie's shoulders, as though to shield them from harm. He was the one calling the shots now.

"Daughter?" The older man choked as though he'd had one cigarette too many. "Girlfriend?" This was getting more interesting by the minute. "Really now?" *Well,* he thought, *it appeared they had a slight problem. What was he going to do about that?*

His hands roamed her body. His lips suckled on her breasts, her neck, and then her face and finally her lips. The sexual tension was mounting between Lissa and Christian. They couldn't get enough of each other. One thing she felt for sure, they'd been in this position before. Maybe more than once, maybe only once. He made her feel so good, with his hands and mouth caressing and exploring her body.

He entered her at exactly the right moment, just before she climaxed. He was a perfectionist in his lovemaking to her. They moved with each other with ease, pleasing each other at exactly the right moments. She was getting hot, very hot.

She heard a key in the door and woke up.

"Why is it so hot in here?" Christian said as he opened the door.

How'd he get a key? Lissa wondered. He was right about the heat. Maybe she hadn't been fully coherent when she'd adjusted the heat earlier. The fireplace was still on too.

Taking the initiative, Christian shut off the fireplace and turned down the heat.

"Were you cold?" he asked. He was concerned, hoping she didn't have a fever, wasn't getting sick. He should check her vitals.

"Yes." She blushed, not sure if it was from the excessive heat in the house or her dream.

"Are you okay?" He felt her forehead.

"As good as can be expected," she said, throwing the comforter off.

"Do you want to go for a drive? Let the house cool off." He thought he'd be sick if he stayed in the house any longer. It was like a sauna.

Lissa contemplated that, wondering if it was a good idea to go anywhere with this man. "Where to?"

"Downtown, to where I found you. Maybe you'll remember something if you go back there."

"Okay." The heat in the house was getting to her as well.

Five minutes later, they were in his car heading downtown. She was intrigued that he drove the same kind of car as his brother. The same color too. *Coincidence, I think not.*

"Is it a coincidence that you drive the same kind of car as your brother, and the same color?"

"He drives the same kind of car as I do, the same color."

What did he mean by that? she wondered. At least Christian wasn't as reckless a driver as his brother was.

CHAPTER EIGHT

Christian parked the car a block away from where he had found her. He figured they could use the fresh air. They were silent as they walked toward the alley.

Lissa grew uneasy as they neared the alley. Numerous homeless people stared at them, no doubt wondering why a middle-class couple was walking in their territory. Some of the homeless were pushing carts down the sidewalk, while others sat on the sidewalk, their hands out. Lissa guessed that any money they got would be spent on drugs or alcohol, rather than a hot meal or a decent place to sleep, at least for one night.

She wondered why and how people ended this way. She shook her head and without even realizing, drew closer to Christian. Thinking she was nervous, he put a protective arm around her waist.

He kissed her forehead, and they continued on their way. "This is where I found you," he whispered to her, pointing to a spot near a dumpster behind a pizza parlor.

Horror struck her. She couldn't believe her luck that he'd found her, let alone seen her from the sidewalk. He would have had to turn off the main street and into the alley to have seen her. What was this man up to? What was he hiding? What was his game?

"Right here?" She pointed to the spot, feeling as though someone was watching them, her. She whipped around and saw a bag lady staring at them. Her face, hands, and clothes were covered in dirt. Her hair was so greasy and dirty, it looked like mud. She must have lived on the streets for years. Her face was hard, with lines from tough living carved into it. She could have been beautiful once. What had happened to her that she had ended up homeless?

Daringly, she walked away from Christian and toward the woman. Her throat tightened, her body became numb. She felt as though she had known the woman from a different life, a different world. The closer Lissa got to the woman, who continued to stare intently at her, the more the woman backed away from her. She left the alley and turned onto the main street.

"I won't hurt you," Lissa said. "I just want to see your face." She didn't know why the woman compelled her so much, she just did.

Just as Lissa placed a hand on the woman's hand, Christian rounded the corner to see where she'd gone. His appearance scared the bag lady, and she ran in the other direction.

"Why did you walk away?" he asked Lissa. "I was worried."

She hadn't thought about that. She just had wanted to get a better look at the woman. She had looked about sixty, but could have been in her forties. Lissa guessed the streets could do that to someone. She wondered what the woman looked like without all the dirt all over her face.

As she and Christian walked away, she kept looking back to see if she could see the woman. She wondered what would have happened had Christian not appeared when he had.

"We scored pizza, Moe," one homeless man yelled to another from down the street.

At least they'd have one good meal that day, Lissa thought. She wished she'd thought to bring her purse to give them some money for food, or to make a phone call so they could reach out and touch someone.

Christian's phone rang as they drove away. He answered, immediately asking, "Do you have something?"

"Nothing conclusive," Liam said. "I was thinking of taking a look around the Manelli cabin to see if I can see something. It seems it could be a good hideout for a baby, at least for a short time."

It was getting dark when Lissa and Christian returned to her house. They were both hungry and tired. He had been up in excess of twenty-four hours, having worked the previous night and been up all that day. He didn't want to sleep, though. He was driven by the need to help Lissa remember her past, get her memory back, and to find their missing son. But he'd have to get some sleep soon or he'd collapse.

He cooked chicken on the grill, and made a salad and rice from what he found in her fridge and cupboards. She hadn't been starving herself, and wouldn't starve with the amount of food she had stocked in her kitchen. She had enough food to feed the homeless in all of Vancouver and then some.

"So you cook?" This intrigued Lissa. Neither Pete nor her father seemed like the types to cook. It was nice having someone take care of her.

"Yes, I cook," he admitted, not embarrassed by the fact.

Brownie points for him. Lissa smiled while they ate. He leafed through some of his textbooks while they did. What was there about this guy? He seemed like a man from another planet, the way he was with her, the things he did and didn't do.

"You don't remember anything at all before you woke up at the hospital this morning?" he asked.

"Nothing," she replied between mouthfuls of chicken. She could mention her dreams, but she thought those were irrelevant and had nothing to do with her missing baby. Then there was the bag lady who had compelled her. She supposed she'd been hoping the woman could help jog her memory or tell her something they could use to help them find the baby, but that was just wishful thinking.

"Are you sure?" Christian asked.

"I'm sure," she said, but wondered if she really was. "Do you blame me for the baby being kidnapped?" She was positive now that her child had been kidnapped. They had searched the area where Christian had found her thoroughly, and hadn't seen any signs of a baby having been there.

"I don't know what happened to you," he said, "so of course I don't blame you." It was true. It wasn't as though she'd given birth to their son on the streets of Vancouver and then gotten up and walked away. He knew in his heart that she wanted this baby as much as he did. He was pretty much convinced that someone had attacked her and kidnapped the baby. And he had a sneaky suspicion that he knew at least two of the people involved.

"I wish I would remember."

"You will." He was as sure of that as he was sure the sun would rise the next day, even in Vancouver. "It may take some time." He hoped not too long. Their child's life was at stake. "Anything at all you think of, even if it seems irrelevant, you have to tell me. It may seem like nothing to you, but it could be something we can build on."

He would have continued, but a knock on the door interrupted him. As he got up to go to the door, Lissa's phone rang. She stared blankly at the caller ID. The name meant nothing to her, but she had to answer. A young woman's voice came on the line. "How are you doing, Lissa?"

"Oh, as good as you could expect." *And who are you?* What else could she say to the stranger on the other end of the phone?

"It's Shellee; I'm your best friend," the woman said. "I'm so sorry to hear about the baby, but you and Christian will find him. I know you will." Shellee was positive of this. If she knew her brother at all, he wouldn't stop until he found their bouncing baby boy.

"We don't really have any leads," Lissa said. "There have been no calls for ransom, no calls at all, no leads, nothing." She was beginning to think the search for her missing baby was hopeless.

"Something will turn up. I'm sure of it. And remember, he loves you, and he'll do everything in his power to find the baby."

"Who loves me?" Lissa was confused now.

"Christian. Who else?"

Lissa was about to answer, when she heard static on the line and then another woman say, "I'll talk to her now, Shellee."

Lissa didn't know what to think. Shellee told Lissa she'd call her later, and then the other woman spoke. "Hello, Lissa. This is Laurel Lynley."

The woman sounded prissy, yet had an edge to her voice. This must be Christian and Pete's mother, she thought. Knowing this woman could one day become an integral part of her life—or maybe already was—she decided to be polite.

"Hi, Laurel." She tried to smile, but couldn't force it.

"How are you doing?"

Lissa wanted to ask her how she thought she was doing, but refrained from the rudeness she wanted to indulge in.

"I'm so sorry," Laurel said quickly. "I didn't think before asking that. Is Pete there with you?"

"No." She wondered where Laurel was going with this conversation.

"Oh? Why not?"

"I don't know where he is." And she didn't. Last she'd heard, he was going to look for the baby, and that was hours ago. She didn't think he was at the door with Christian. That looked more like her father. "Christian is here," she said. After hearing what sounded like a growl on the other end of the line, she wondered if maybe she shouldn't have told Laurel that.

"Why is he there?" Laurel demanded.

"He's trying to help me."

"Pete should be the one there, the one helping. Christian should stay out of it."

"Why is that?" Lissa rubbed her head. Another headache brewing. Suddenly, she felt very uncomfortable talking to this woman, even though she was hundreds of miles away.

"He's the father of your baby," Laurel said smugly.

"And how do you know that?"

"I just do. And so do you, even if you don't remember it right now. But you will. Pete is the father of your baby, not Christian. You and Pete were together when your baby was conceived."

Had she watched them have sex? Did she have a magnifying glass that saw through the skin so that she could watch the egg meet sperm?

Everything she'd been told by everyone that day spun through her mind. She wondered who was lying, or if anyone was telling her the truth. She couldn't take it anymore. She dropped the phone and turned. Christian and her father were standing right there, and Christian caught her as she passed out cold.

CHAPTER NINE

The following day, Saturday, Lissa, Christian, and Liam took a trip to the mountains to the cabin, owned by Lissa's father, that Liam had found. Their thinking was that the kidnappers might be using the cabin as a hideout. The only other property in the Vancouver area that Liam had found was a cottage on Vancouver Island, which was a possibility too. They would check that out if the cabin turned out to be a dead end.

Christian drove with Lissa beside him in the front, Liam in the back. It was about an hour's drive from her house to the cabin, giving Lissa plenty of time to think about the previous night.

When she had come to, not only were her father and Christian there, but Pete as well. He was distraught at her condition and demanded she go back to the hospital. He appeared genuinely worried about her.

"She'll be fine," Christian said. "I'm a medical professional. I know how to treat her."

Darn right she wasn't going back to the hospital, Lissa thought, annoyed at both Pete and Christian for trying to say what was best for her. If they did take her back, she wouldn't stay anyway. She'd get out, same as she had before.

Her father had added to her stress, trying to call the shots and take charge, attempting to get the other men out of the house. It had been a no-win situation for Lissa. Finally, she had grown tired of the commotion and gone upstairs to bed, yelling for them all to get out of her house before slamming her door.

She went back down when the house was quiet. Checking the window, she saw no cars in her driveway. In the living room, she sat down on the couch, and only then did she let the tears fall, fall harder than Niagara Falls. She didn't know how long she sat there crying when Christian returned to get the textbooks he had forgotten. When he saw her sobbing, he sat beside her and drew her into his arms, kissed her forehead, and let her cry until she fell asleep.

She was vaguely aware of him carrying her to bed and lying beside her, running his hand through her hair and across her shoulders and back. When she woke in the morning, she was alone.

Pete came over a little while after she got up, to tell her he didn't have any news about the baby, but that he wasn't giving up, not by a long shot.

"How come your mother hates me so much?" she asked. Had she done something Laurel didn't like? Was she mad that Lissa had been pregnant with one of her son's baby, and now he or she had gone missing? Was that it?

"She doesn't hate you, love bug," Pete assured her. "She's upset about the kidnapping and is sick and tired of my brother trying to interfere with our relationship, claiming he's the father when he knows damn well he's not."

"Shellee said that it was always Christian and me, and that he's the father of my baby."

"She hates me, they both hate me. She's lying. She and Christian have always been tied at the hip. They might as well be twins, they're so close."

Lissa cooked fried eggs and bacon while she thought over what he'd said. She couldn't imagine hating a sibling of hers and had heard that she was close to her brother, as close as Christian and Shellee were.

"Why do they hate you so much?" she asked Pete. "Or is it that you hate them?"

Pete sat in silence as he ate. Lissa smiled, wondering if she'd touched a nerve. Was there more to Pete's story than she knew? Where had he gone yesterday? And where was Christian? She didn't know where he'd gone either, or even when he'd even left her house.

They finished breakfast. As Lissa was loading the dishwasher, Pete approached her, took the dishes from her hands, and placed them on the counter.

He gave her a bear hug, almost squeezing too hard. He ran his hands down her front and smiled at her lovingly. Pushing her against the counter, his body as close as he could get to hers, he gave her a mouth-watering kiss. Their hips pressed close together, they both felt his reaction.

Lissa noticed he wasn't as cold as he had been the previous day. *Maybe he was human after all.*

She found herself enjoying their kiss as their hunger for each other grew. His hands slid under her shirt and undid her bra, and then caressed her breasts as their kisses grew more passionate.

"I love you, Lissa," he said, slightly out of breath, while his hands continued to explore her body. "You love me, too, and very soon you are going to realize that."

She smiled at him as she ran her hands up his back. "You know . . ." She hesitated, not sure if she should say what she wanted to, but she desperately wanted him. She had the distinct feeling he felt the same way.

"What's that, babe?" he asked in a voice so soft, it made her melt for him more.

"I think we should wait."

His eyes glazed over hurt by her words and he turned away.

She tried reassuring him, she wanted him to know he misunderstood, "Pete,". but she was interrupted by the phone ringing. It was Christian, telling her he and Liam were coming over to pick her up for the drive to the cabin. Pete left before his brother got there and before she explained her reasons of not wanting to be intimate with him.

Lissa glanced at Christian in the driver's seat. "Why does your mother hate me so much?" She hadn't gotten much out of Pete. What would Christian's story be?

He sighed. "It's long and depressing." He wasn't trying to stall her, just trying to think of where to start.

"Humor me," she said. She glanced at Liam. "Or rather, us."

"For some cockamamie reason, she believes that Pete is the father of our baby. He probably planted that idea in her head. She thinks that the two of you belong together, not us and that you two made a baby, not us." He had given up trying to understand his mother's thinking regarding his brother years ago.

"Wouldn't she be happy for you and me?"

"You'd think," Christian said with anger in his voice. "Pete has her wrapped around his little finger. She believes everything he tells her, and everyone else is a liar." He resented it in his own way, but in the end he'd be the winner, Pete would be the loser, and maybe then his mother would see what her precious son was all about.

"The cabin isn't too far from here, Christian," Liam said, checking his map and their surroundings. They were in the mountains now, the ocean below them.

Christian smiled as he turned into the driveway.

It was starting to rain, so it was a good thing they had come equipped with raincoats and rubber boots. There were no cars in the driveway. The cabin was made of wood, like something you would see on *Little House on the Prairie*. The driveway was made of gravel; there were muddy areas and puddles everywhere.

The pine trees surrounding them looked as though they'd been there longer than the cabin. Despite the forest of trees, they could hear the ocean roaring below them.

Liam knocked on the door; no answer. He tried opening the door, but it was locked. One slip of a credit card opened the door, releasing more pine smell and the stench of cigarettes.

"Nice," Christian said. "Smoking in the house with a newborn."

"We don't even know if he's here, or was here," Lissa said.

Christian was keenly aware that she had said "he." Perhaps she was beginning to believe him. "I'm sure he's been here," he said. Just a gut feeling he had. Walking around the two-room cabin, he looked for signs that a baby had been there. But there was no crib or cradle, no playpen, no baby seat, no toys, rattles, clothes, nothing at all, except for a single baby bottle.

"Maybe the kidnappers are already gone and took everything with them," Liam said.

They locked the door on the way out and went around the back. The rain was coming down in sheets now. They peeked through the garage window but saw only blank walls and a concrete floor with tires tracks on it.

Christian instantly wondered how new the tire tracks were. He tried to open the door, but it was an automatic. It could only be opened by a remote or from the inside of the garage. They could try to disable the mechanism, but it would be pointless. They probably wouldn't be able to tell how new or old the tracks were unless they were wet, and they could have belonged to anyone, even Phillip Manelli.

They hurried back to the car, eager to get out of the heavy rain. Had it not been for the rain or the roaring of the ocean, one, two, or all of them might have heard a baby's incessant crying, a cry for its mother.

Lissa broke down in the car. She'd put all of her hopes in this one lead. She didn't know what she'd expected by coming to the cabin, but a part of her had expected to find her baby at the cabin. He would be here waiting for her, wondering why it had taken her so long to get there.

Who was she kidding? He probably thought the person or people who were looking after him were his parents. He was only a day and a half old. Who could blame him? She hoped whoever had him was looking after him. By the time she got him back, and she would, he wouldn't know her, and would probably cry for his previous mother. Oh, God!

"Come here." Christian guided her to him to hug her, comfort her. "It's only one lead, and we didn't even know for sure this was a lead. It was a hunch. We're going to find him."

She pulled away then, unsure if she wanted his comfort. She began wondering if it were wishful thinking that they would find the baby.

"Don't give up hope," Christian said. "This is just the beginning." He knew in his heart it was, but at the same time he hoped a clue would come their way, and that not too much time would pass before they found their son.

"It's hard," Lissa sobbed.

Liam placed a comforting hand on her shoulder from the back seat. "Just a fly-by-night," he said, "but do you want to check out that island cottage?"

"Yeah, what do we have to lose?" *Except time,* Christian thought. He rubbed a hand over his face in frustration. It was a two-and-a-half-hour ferry ride each way. He wished he could have a smoke, but he never smoked in his car. On the ferry, he could have one. "Do you want to go, Leigh?"

She shrugged. Tears continued streaming down her face.

Christian figured her shrug meant she wasn't opposed to the idea. "Okay, to the cottage we go." He knew where it was. He and Lissa had been there countless times.

They drove on in silence. No one said a word on the way to the ferry. When they arrived, they were fifth in line. Christian got out to check the time for the next ferry, even though he already knew, and to have a smoke. He needed something to ward off his rising anxiety, or he was going to crack. He wanted to stay strong for Lissa.

Following Christian's lead, Lissa took a cigarette out of the glove box and stepped out of the car. She didn't know if she had smoked in her previous life, but it looked like a good idea.

Christian watched her and debated if he should go talk to her, or just leave her be. Thus far, it had been an emotional day, and it wasn't over yet. He figured she needed a few minutes to herself and opted to leave her alone, for now.

Smoking the cigarette felt natural to Lissa, so she figured she had been a smoker in her past life. She wondered if she had smoked during her pregnancy, and certainly hoped she hadn't. She knew that smoking during pregnancy resulted in low birth weight, increased heartbeat, breathing issues, increased risk of death, and so much more. She choked on a sob, thinking of the damage she could've done to her newborn baby, whom she had yet to hold in her arms and tell him how much she loved him.

Hearing her sobbing, Christian ran to her, "What is it?" he asked, putting his arm around her.

"Do I smoke?" She cried against his shoulder.

"Yeah, you've been known to smoke."

"What about during my pregnancy?"

"I don't think you smoked very much during the pregnancy. I know you had one about a month ago, but you told me you hadn't had one for awhile."

That eased her conscience a little bit, but not much. She threw the unfinished cigarette into the ocean and turned to go back to the car. The ferry was almost in.

During the ferry ride, Lissa leaned against the railing and watched the ocean, watched the islands sail by them. Christian and Liam stayed in the car and talked about what they knew and where to go from here.

Christian kept eyeing Lissa from time to time to see if she'd moved, if she was talking to anyone, and most of all, if she was still aboard. He didn't think she'd jump overboard, but he was beginning to worry about her state of mind.

They really needed to continue trying to restore her memory. Maybe later, once they got back from the island, she'd be game for that.

"I'm really worried about her," Christian told Liam, getting out another cigarette from the glove box.

"I am too. You know, smoking isn't going to help. It isn't going to help find your baby."

Christian sighed. "Yeah, I know, but it's a stress reliever." So he told himself. He got out the car and walked around to the other side of the ferry, away from Lissa but within sight. As he lit up his cigarette, he saw that she was having another one too. Like mother, like father. She must have taken another from his glove compartment or had some in her purse.

It was only a short drive to the cottage from the dock, about fifteen minutes. Christian had a key for the cottage in his car. Neither Lissa nor Liam asked why he had the key and where it had come from.

The cottage was on the Pacific Ocean. It was two stories with white siding, and a porch that went all the way around the house.

All of the windows were open, as though someone was living there. They all found that very interesting, but like the cabin, no cars occupied the driveway.

"Hello," Christian called out as he opened the door and walked in. There were papers and a laptop on the kitchen table, coffee in the coffee pot, dishes in the sink. Christian walked over and felt the pot. Lukewarm.

Lissa walked around the house while Liam leafed through the papers on the table and Christian turned on the laptop. It was, unfortunately, password protected. He turned his attention to the cupboards and fridge, to see how much food was on hand, while he thought about what password Phillip Manelli would use.

"No one's here." Lissa's voice was barely audible when she rejoined them in the kitchen. She was exhausted.

That was good for them, for the time being. Christian and Liam kept looking through the papers, which related to business deals in Dubai, France, the United States, and Canada. There were bank statements and bills, and invoices for a business called Busy Babes.

"Busy Babes?" Christian muttered. "What the hell is that?"

"Someone's coming," Lissa whispered.

Christian almost asked her who it was, then realized that would be pointless unless it was her father. "Is it your father?"

"No, a woman with blond hair."

Christian turned toward the window to see if he knew who it was. "Looks like Cassie Manelli," he said. "Your stepmother." He didn't know what they should do, grab the papers and run out the back, or meet her on the front porch to have a friendly conversation.

He doubted she knew anything about the kidnapping.

"How harmless is she?" Liam asked Christian.

"Not very. She'll probably make us lunch, be happy to have us for guests. But then she'll also ask us to stay for supper—with her husband. Even if we don't stay, I guarantee she'll tell her husband we were here. He'll figure we were snooping around and he won't like that."

Christian slipped the most relevant papers in his jacket and contemplated what to do They had about one minute to decide whether to make a run for it or meet her on the porch with the door locked, acting as though they had not been inside.

"You said I've never had much of a relationship with her?" Lissa said. She watched the other woman, who was taking her time getting to the house, just looking around, checking out the view.

"No, not really," Christian said. "You father never advocated a relationship between his kids and their stepmother."

Lissa wasn't sure she wanted to deal with yet another person's sympathy over the kidnapping of her baby, especially a stepmother she didn't have a relationship with. "Let's go." Decision made, she was out the door in a second.

"Okay then," Christian said. "That settles that." On impulse he grabbed the laptop on their way out. He could probably figure out the password; it probably had something to do with Lissa. The men quickly followed her to the car, checking to see how far Cassie was from the house and if she would see them. He threw the car keys at Lissa; she caught them without looking. He shook his head in glee. So typical of her.

The car was out of sight, behind the end of the driveway, by the time Cassie reached the house. If she had seen them, she would've waved them down, tried to stop them. Phillip had gone to get lunch, and then they were going back to the city. He had some business there. Even on weekends he didn't stop. He never ceased to amaze his wife.

Five minutes later, Phillip was back at the cottage, smiling, lunch in his hand. The first thing he noticed was that his papers and laptop were gone from the kitchen table. "Baby," he called, "did you move my papers from the table?" Who else would've moved them?

"Yes," she answered from upstairs. "It's lunchtime. You can't eat and work." Her voice got closer as she came downstairs. "You think we can wait awhile longer before going back to the city?" She appeared in the doorway to the kitchen wearing a black negligee.

"I think lunch can wait too." He pulled her into his arms and kissed her, then scooped her up and carried her up the stairs to their bed. "I love you," he breathed in her ear.

CHAPTER TEN

Christian handed the papers to Liam while Lissa drove. She found she could easily drive a standard. Just like riding a bike. "I can't believe you stole those papers and laptop," she said in awe.

"Don't think of it as stealing," Christian said. "Think of it as borrowing."

"We're going to return them," Liam said.

"Before he notices they're gone?" she asked, disbelieving. A workaholic would absolutely notice missing paperwork and a laptop.

Christian laughed. "We can only hope."

"You really think my father had something to do with our son's kidnapping?" Lissa asked as she got in line for the ferry back to the city. Christian didn't answer.

Where was he dragging her now? Lissa wondered, drumming her hands on the steering wheel as she drove through the countryside on the other side of Vancouver. They had been gone for hours, and she was tired and hungry. The least they could have done was stop for takeout rather than starve themselves. What was with all the secrets all of the sudden?

"We're not far now," Christian informed her after going through the last of the papers.

"Where are we going?" What was Christian keeping from her? He had made a number of calls along the way, but had not revealed who he was calling and why.

"We are going to see your brother."

"Oh." *More sympathy. When would it end?*

Chad was shorter than Christian, about five seven, and slender. He had auburn-colored hair with bluish green eyes. He was waiting for them in the parking lot of the rehab center when they arrived. As soon as Lissa got out of the car, Chad wrapped his arms around her in a bear hug, tears running down his face. He'd missed her more than life itself.

Sensing his sister was uncomfortable and maybe didn't remember him, he sheepishly pulled away and said in a cracked voice, "I'm sorry." He looked at her face. "You don't remember me, do you?" Tears again filled his eyes. His best friend, the one person he could always count on, didn't even know who he was. He'd hoped that seeing him would trigger a memory in her, something, anything. But Christian hadn't triggered anything inside her either, and he'd been her closest friend for so long.

Christian was disappointed as well.

The four of them stood awkwardly in the middle of the parking lot, each pondering what to say.

"I'm sorry," Lissa said. Tears filled her eyes as well. "I wish I did." Christian had told her how close she and her brother were.

"I'm sorry about you and the baby, Lissa," Chad said. "We will find him, though."

Lissa nodded and gave him a half smile.

"Hungry?" Chad asking, sensing her growling stomach.

She nodded. They started for the rehab center, and then Chad grabbed her hand and whispered in her ear, "He's the father of your baby, your son."

She immediately wondered if he was lying. How could he know. Could she trust anyone anymore?

Chad kissed her on the check and whispered, "I love you."

Christian asked her on the way inside what Chad had said to her. She didn't answer.

They sat down in the dining room and ate roast chicken, mashed potatoes, gravy, rolls, salad, peas, carrots, chocolate cake, and ice cream. There wasn't an empty stomach between them after the last bite.

They chatted amicably while they ate, and Lissa looked through family photo albums that Chad had brought out, hoping they would refresh her memory. They didn't.

Afterwards they went to the library, out of earshot of the other residents and their visitors. The men pored through the laptop files and papers while Lissa half listened absorbed in her own thoughts. Liam and Christian were able to reboot the laptop into safe mode and remove the password from the account settings.

"Do you know anything about any illegal dealings your father may be working on?" Christian asked Chad.

"He's barely said ten words to me in the six months I've been here," Chad said.

Or maybe, Lissa thought, *he was involved in this as well. Christian already thought their father was involved. What if this strained relationship between father and son was just a ploy?*

"However," Chad went on, "when I was in Dad's office before we came here, I did hear part of a strange conversation."

"Strange how?" Christian asked.

"It may not even be relevant," Chad said, "and I can't remember the exact words. But basically he said, 'Nobody can know about this, nobody. Not my wife, my daughter, my son, my brother, no one. It'll take place upon birth and nothing will go wrong, nothing. No one can or will ever know, just like in the past. You know what happened to my ex when she messed with me. I'll give you what you want for a price.'" Chad shook his head. "It's not much and it doesn't get us any closer to finding your son. It doesn't even prove he was involved."

The men discussed what Chad had overheard, and then went back to the papers and laptop. Lissa quietly slipped away. When Christian finally looked up and noticed she was gone, an hour had passed.

"Where the hell did she go and how long has she been gone?" She had the car keys, and he hoped she hadn't taken off. She didn't know where she was going—unless she had suddenly remembered.

Rushing outside, he found his suspicions had been correct. His car was indeed gone.

Lissa found her way without too much trouble. After a few wrong turns, she ended up downtown near the alley where Christian had found her. She parked the car and walked to the alley, hoping to see the homeless woman she'd seen the day before.

"Whatcha doing down here, little girl?" a homeless man asked her, and smacked his lips. He was obviously chewing tobacco, and from the looks of his browner-than-mud teeth, had been doing it for a long time. He was in a bad need of a toothbrush, toothpaste, and mouthwash.

"Looking for someone I know." She wasn't afraid. At least she told herself that.

"Don't think you know anyone from this neighborhood." He chuckled and then broke into an uncontrollable cough.

"You'd be surprised," she mumbled.

"What they look like?" he asked.

"Brownish hair, maybe with some auburn in it." It had been hard to tell from all that dirt covering her.

"M—" he started, and then abruptly stopped when he broke into another cough, this one worse than the last.

Lung cancer, Lissa thought. She turned around and ran smack into Christian, who had a disapproving look on his face.

Lissa's answering machine was blinking when they got home. She pressed play.

"Lissa, this is Ross Marler. I'm your uncle. We need to talk about the baby. I'm a lawyer, you know. I talked to Christian and he wants to make some arrangements and—"

Lissa stabbed the stop button and whirled on Christian. *What the hell did he think he was doing?*

"What the fuck was that about?" she asked.

"What?" Christian didn't understand why she was so upset. All he'd done was call Ross to ask him if he knew anything about Phillip's recent business dealings. Phillip and Ross weren't that close, but he still handled some of his business deals. "What do you think that was about?"

"You want custody of a baby that we don't have and may not be yours," she yelled. "There's a strong possibility that it's your brother's." As she started trusting Christian less, she was starting to believe Pete more. Where was he anyway?

"Oh, the baby is mine all right. And I called your uncle to see if he could shed any light on what Chad overheard."

"Oh," was all she could say, embarrassed by her misinterpretation.

"I wouldn't take custody away from you. We can work out arrangements for me to see our son when *we* get him back, if we can't work things out between us."

"Now, I want you to close your eyes," Christian ordered her an hour later while she lay on the couch. Christian was hoping they could make some progress with her memory.

Lissa wondered if there was any point to this. Would they gain anything from it? Would she remember anything? She was beginning to lose faith in regaining her memory or finding her baby. She had just about lost faith in everything.

Unfortunately, exhaustion consumed her, and she fell asleep before they barely got started. Christian realized she was asleep when she didn't respond to his questions. He figured he might as well try to make some progress elsewhere and left quietly.

The sound of the door opening roused her, and she opened her eyes to see Pete bending down to give her a kiss. Prince Charming waking Sleeping Beauty.

He barely had his lips on hers when she reared back and sat up.

"Where the hell have you been all day?" he asked.

"Trying to get some leads." She left it at that, not sure how much to tell him.

He sat close to her, rubbing her legs and back, and finally urging her close enough to give her a deep and emotional kiss.

His lips were warmer still than that morning, almost hot. It felt good, and she felt arousal building in every inch of her body. She wanted him and wanted him badly. But she knew she couldn't., sheepishly she pulled away.

"We can't, it's too soon," she painfully told him. She wondered if it was because it was so soon after giving birth or her jagged feelings for him.

Pete's dismay was read on his face. "You're amazing," he whispered attempting to coax her. "I love you."

"Ah . . ." Lissa stammered. How could she say those words back when she didn't even know who she was, didn't know if she trusted him or not? She didn't know what their relationship really had been in the past. If she listened to her body and the way it was responding to him, she could almost believe he was the one she loved and who had fathered her child, not Christian.

Her hesitation seemed to have killed the moment. Pete jumped up off the couch and stared at her, looking upset.

"I'm sorry." *What had she said?* She tried to pull him back on the couch with her, but he turned away as he had earlier.

Damn, Pete thought. *What the hell had he just done?* The one woman in the world he loved and wanted more than life, and he had turned away from her.

He was the father of her baby, she was the love of his life, he was the love of her life; and he had turned away from her because she didn't reciprocate his words of love. All she had said in return was, "ah."

What was wrong with him? The woman had amnesia and didn't remember him and had just given birth to their missing child.

CHAPTER ELEVEN

The sound of the doorbell startled Lissa as she wandered aimlessly around her house. She was going from room to room, looking for something that could help trigger a memory. Who could be ringing her bell at six o'clock on a Saturday night? Christian or Pete would just come in. Her father was at a business dinner. She knew because he had called earlier to check in on her, see how she was, and see if there was anything he could do for her.

She had been expecting a lonely Saturday night with nothing but her thoughts and blank mind.

She opened the door, and if she hadn't known better, she would've thought the woman standing there was her mother. But she knew her mother was dead and still didn't know how she had died. She should've asked her brother. The thought hadn't crossed her mind at the time.

The woman at the door was the same height as Lissa, with sunflower blonde hair shaped into a bob, shiny blue eyes that sparkled, and a figure every woman desired. She looked thirty, although Christian had told her she was in her forties. She was casually dressed in designer blue jeans and a blue sweater that accentuated her eyes.

Was Cassie Manelli the wicked stepmother from the west? Lissa wasn't sure of that theory yet. Christian had told her she was a very nice woman, too good for her father, and that she and Lissa didn't have much of a relationship. Much to her dismay, Christian suspected it had to do with her doting father.

"Hi, Lissa." Cassie smiled and gave her a hug.

"Cassie?"

"Oh, I'm so sorry," Cassie said. "I should've introduced myself, maybe called to say that I'd like to come over."

"No, no, it's fine," Lissa assured her. She was happy for the diversion, someone new to talk to, maybe find out some new things about her life and the people in it.

"I came over to see if I could offer you a shoulder to cry on, or lean on."

Cassie had come without her husband's knowledge, as he forbade her from contacting his daughter. The day before he had ordered her to, "stay away from my daughter. You can't help her. She doesn't know you, you don't know her."

"Whose fault is that?" she'd dared to snap back at him.

He snarled at her and left the room.

Cassie had never understood why Phillip hadn't encouraged her to have a relationship with his children. Instead he'd discouraged it, forbidden it even. When their mother passed away a few years after she and Phillip married, she had wanted them to come and live with them. His response had been, "No way in hell They're teenagers who live in the city. They have their own lives and friends, We can't relocate them into the country. Either they'll go crazy or we will." It made no sense to her, but she knew that once her husband's mind was made up, he wouldn't relent.

"How are you doing, Lissa?" she asked her stepdaughter. She sensed the pain Lissa felt. They sat down on the couch, and Cassie lightly touched Lissa's arm.

Lissa shrugged in response. She didn't really know how she felt, other than exhausted and numb all over.

"What do you know about my boyfriends, the father of my baby?" Cassie had to know something. She couldn't imagine her father had completely alienated his wife from his children's lives.

"Boyfriend," Cassie corrected. "You were always interested in one boy and one boy only since you were a teenager."

The anticipation was killing her. She only hoped his woman wasn't feeding her more lies. She didn't know what or who to believe anymore.

"Christian," Cassie said, "was your only boyfriend seven years. You lived together for almost four years with his sister, Shellee."

"I see." Or did she?

Cassie went on. "I don't believe for one second that you ever slept with Pete, or anyone else for that matter."

Phillip would kill her if he knew where she was right now and what she was doing, but Cassie felt Lissa deserved and needed to know what she was telling her. It was high time someone told her the truth for a change, other than Christian, and she had a feeling that under the circumstances, Lissa wouldn't believe what Christian told her.

"Stay away from Pete," Cassie continued. "Pardon my French, but calling him an asshole is too mild of a name for him." She'd heard stories about Pete, and she hadn't liked what she'd heard.

Lissa contemplated what she'd said. Pete hadn't seemed that bad to her, but looks and words could be deceiving. When she thought about it, she didn't really know too much about him. She actually didn't know too much about any of them.

Feeling uncomfortable with the subject and needing to know more about other aspects of her life, Lissa abruptly changed the subject. "How did my mother die?"

"In a fire when you were thirteen."

Cassie saw an odd expression cross Lissa's face. "Something wrong?"

"No, no." Flashbacks of her dream ran through her head.

Cassie wasn't convinced, but let it be. The last thing she wanted to do was pressure her in her tenuous state. Maybe it was time for a new topic. This one seemed to make her uncomfortable, and Cassie suspecting there was something Lissa wasn't saying that maybe she should.

"What can I do to help?" She leaned closer to Lissa, and as she did, the clasp on her necklace gave way. Her locket fell to the floor.

Lissa was quicker at picking it up than Cassie was. "May I?" she politely asked, holding the locket in her hand.

Cassie smiled and nodded.

Lissa opened the locket and looked at its contents. "Is that your daughter?" Lissa smiled at the face of the tiny infant.

"Yes, her name is Bessie."

Instead of a picture on the other side of the locket, Lissa saw a question mark. "Why is there a question mark there?"

Cassie looked away, but not before Lissa saw tears fill her eyes. Obviously, she had opened up some old wounds. "I'm so sorry. I didn't mean to pry. We can talk about something else."

"I I lost a baby."

Cassie would have gone on, but they both heard a key in the door.

Christian walked in. He seemed surprised to see Cassie. He started to greet her, but then seemed to sense the tension between the two women.

"Is something wrong?" he asked.

Cassie and Lissa looked at each other, and neither uttered a word.

"So that was a nice surprise to see Cassie here," Christian said after Cassie was gone. He wasn't going to pry and ask what they had been talking about, but he could tell it had been emotional. His arriving at that time had been either good fortune for them or bad timing on his part.

Lissa smiled and said nothing. She went upstairs, and a moment later, he heard her scream. He rushed upstairs to see what was wrong.

"What is it?" he asked, panic in his voice.

She was standing in the hall, shaking like a leaf, tears streaming down her pale face,

She pointed to the nursery. "Who would do such a thing?"

Christian walked into the nursery, shocked beyond words by what he saw. "What the hell?" the room was completely empty. Only the carpeting and the four walls remained. Everything in the room had been removed. There were no traces of the contents that had been there. What, who, when, why, how? He had his theories who. *They were going to pay,* he promised as he returned to a distraught Lissa in the hall.

He pulled a sobbing Lissa into his arms, not only so he could console her, but so she could console him as well. This was their battle. They were in this together until the end. She held onto him for dear life.

He broke their embrace, took her hand, and led her into her bedroom. They lay down on the bed and wrapped their arms around each other.

Lissa settled down after a few minutes and closed her eyes. Christian rubbed her back and shoulders, and then ran his hand through her silky blond hair. She moaned softly, apparently enjoying his caressing.

Moments later their lips were hungrily on each others kissing as though they had never kissed before. Their lips were hot on the others and they could feel the sizzling of their bodies. They smiled at each other in the darkness after the kiss wanting more, but knowing they weren't ready yet to cross the next bridge. They had other bridges to cross first.

Lissa was almost asleep when she mumbled, "I love you, Lyn."

Christian's head popped up in amazement. He had longed to hear those words from her again. "I love you, Leigh," but she was already asleep.

CHAPTER TWELVE

Sleepy-eyed and yawning, Lissa opened the door to her father the next morning.

Phillip hugged her tight, while she just lightly wrapped her arms around his shoulders.

Taking a good look at his daughter, he noticed something different about her this morning. She had a kind of glow to her face that she hadn't had the day before. When he saw Christian come down the stairs, he had a feeling he knew why, and he was disappointed in her.

"Good morning," Christian said. He soundly kissed Lissa and then gave Phillip a look, as if to say, May the best man win?

Phillip silently snarled back at him and refocused his attention on his daughter. "We need to talk," he said.

Christian took the hint. "I'm going to take a shower and then we can figure out where to start today." With that, he went back upstairs, whistling.

"Lissa, what the hell are you doing with that scumbag?"

She shrugged. "It's my life. And he could be the father of my baby."

They heard the shower start upstairs.

"And maybe he's not." He hoped and prayed he wasn't. In the meantime, this father only wanted the best for his little girl, which is how he sometimes still thought of Lissa.

"Why are you here?" she asked, sounding annoyed.

"To talk some sense into you. You're smarter than this." She had to listen to reason, just had to. "You are the most important person in my life." *The apple of his eye.* He hesitated, knowing he had to choose his words carefully. "Lissa, I'm a firm believer in everything happening for a reason."

"And the reason for my baby being ripped out from inside of me?"

He again paused. He didn't want to sound too harsh. "It's a sign telling you to finish your education, then find someone worthy of you, and then have a family. These boys aren't worth shit on a stick."

"I want my baby back and I will find him or her."

Phillip sighed and wondered how to convince her otherwise. This amnesia Lissa was just as stubborn as, or even more so, than his precious Lissa was in her right state of mind. When it involved the Lynley boys, though, in his opinion she wasn't in her right state of mind. She definitely had her eyes tightly shut. He had to figure out a way to get them out of her life. But how? Maybe he had to convince her that her baby was gone for good.

"Stop sleeping with these boys and making babies with them!" he shouted at her.

Neither of them had heard the front door open and Pete walk in, but he heard Phillip's words. Was he saying that Lissa had slept with his brother?

Christian came down the stairs at that moment and smiled knowingly at his brother, confirming Pete's worse fears.

He turned on Lissa. "How could you, after everything we've been through and everything's I've told you?" This could be very bad for him. He had to figure out a way to turn this around, in his favor. He had to find the baby. It was the only way.

After Phillip left and Pete had stormed out, Lissa and Christian sat down at the kitchen table to have breakfast. Since they had missed supper the night before, they were both famished.

Christian looked at Lissa. "What aren't you telling me?" He suspected she was keeping something from him, something very important that could be life altering.

I almost slept with your brother. She couldn't tell him that. It would kill him in one of the worst possible ways. The only thing that would be worse for Christian would be if the baby turned out to be his brother's.

"I don't know what you mean," she said. In a way she did, in a way she didn't.

Even with her amnesia, he knew her well enough to know when she was lying.

"What do you want to know?" she asked. "The dream I had, my feelings for you and your brother, how frustrated I am that we haven't found *my* baby yet and that I'm not sure if we ever will." There it was, back to *my* back again.

Back to "my" again, Christian thought. He let that one go. They'd deal with it later. It was "the dream" that caught his attention. "Dream? What dream?" She'd never mentioned anything about a dream.

She told him about the burning house, the boy who was with her, how she'd been pregnant, but then her stomach had deflated and she'd woken up screaming.

"I was the boy with you," he informed her.

Lissa was shocked. "It was real?"

"Your mother died in that fire."

Lissa replayed in her mind yesterday's conversation with Cassie. *She died in a fire.*

"Why didn't you tell me this sooner?"

"I thought it was irrelevant." She still did.

"What else?"

Lissa thought back, wondering if there was something she had missed. She didn't think so.

"Why were you in the alley yesterday?" he asked. "Why did you go back there?"

She sat silent, not touching her breakfast, wondering what to say. "That's where this all started," she said finally. Or so she thought.

"There's more," he said. "Why were you acting unusual in the alley when we were first there?"

"I saw a woman. A woman in my dream called me Ana Lissa, but I never saw her face in the dream." Or had she blocked it out?

Christian got up so fast, he almost tipped his chair onto the floor. This could be the lead they'd been waiting for. This could break the case wide open.

She got up too. "Where are we going?"

"You're staying here." He brushed her lips with a kiss. "I'm going alone on this one. I know your father has something to do with this."

"How dare you accurse him without any proof. I know he doesn't like you. And I have to wonder why."

"I'll tell you why. Because he knows I'm onto him."

"Go do what you have to do then," she snapped. She didn't want to see him anymore. She started to leave the kitchen, having barely touched her breakfast, but he called her back.

"Eat," he said. She scowled at him, and he added, in a gentler voice, "You need to keep your strength up. You haven't eaten since yesterday afternoon."

"Go to hell," she said, and stormed out the back door. "Go do what you have to do." Probably go see their son, if it was even a boy. No, not his son, her son, and only hers. Tears threatened and then fell. "Bastard!" she shouted, and hoped he heard her.

"Where are you?" Christian yelled when he reached his destination. There didn't appear to be anyone around, but he believed people were there. They were just hiding. "I'm here to help you, but I need your help."

After fifteen minutes of walking around and calling out, no one answered, no one appeared.

Just as he was about to give up and leave, a hand reached out and touched his. He whipped around and stared into the most horrifying face he'd ever seen.

"I know where the baby is," the stranger said.

The door to Christian's apartment was unlocked, so she didn't bother knocking. She was still mad at him, but she'd gone there because her child's life was more important than some stupid argument they'd had.

Nice and cozy was her first thought as she glanced around at the apartment. It shouldn't have surprised her to see how tidy it was, but it did. She saw he was on the balcony, his back to her. Rather than announcing her presence, she decided to look around to see if she could find something he could be hiding, any clues that he had kidnapped her baby.

Nothing. After going through the apartment room by room, she hadn't found a shred of evidence that discredited him and proved he was indeed hiding her baby somewhere.

She was about to go find him, when she turned and saw that she had missed what appeared to be a spare room. Opening the door on impulse, she saw a woman sleeping on the bed. She appeared to be naked. A man's robe lay on a chair.

She gaped at the woman. Her first instincts about him had been correct: he wasn't to be trusted. He was hiding something.

He had been lying to her the whole time, and her father had been right about him all along. Why did she wear rose-colored glasses when it came to this man?

Still, the woman seemed familiar to her. As she stared at her, something stirred inside her, drew her to the woman. She needed to get closer look at her.

No. She stopped herself. It didn't matter who the woman was. All that mattered was that she was naked in Christian's apartment. He had probably just slept with her, made mad, passionate love to her. Had he compared this woman's lovemaking to hers had they been intimate before? Maybe the other woman was better in bed than she was.

"Bitch," she muttered, and ran out of the apartment, slamming the door behind her. She didn't care if the noise woke the woman or alerted Christian to her presence.

The woman and Christian rushed into the living room at the same time, the woman dressed in the robe he had left out for her.

Christian had a feeling Lissa had been in the apartment, and he ran out into the hall after her. He was too late. She was long gone or hiding somewhere.

"Leigh!" he called, in case she was in earshot. "It's not what you think. You misunderstood. Please come back and I'll explain everything to you. We'll explain everything to you. There's someone I want you to meet."

Silence, damn it. He went back into his apartment, sat on the couch, and dropped his head into his hands.

"What now?" the woman asked.

Lissa was racing out of the apartment building when her cell phone rang. "Hello," she answered breathlessly.

"I found the baby. I know where the baby is," Pete said excitedly. "I'm parked across the street."

Looking around, she spotted Pete's car. He'd followed her? She'd deal with that later.

"Where is he?" she asked as she got into the car. She didn't care how Pete had found him. All she knew was that she was getting her baby back, and soon he would be in her arms where he belonged.

"We have some driving to do, but we will have our baby in no time," he said, hugging her tight.

She hugged him back and breathlessly kissed him. Suddenly she was sorry for what almost happened with Christian. Pete was the one; Pete was the father. She knew that now.

A surprised Pete didn't fight back, this was a pleasant switch. He mused. He kissed her back with as much force, more force than she was kissing him. Wow!

"I didn't sleep with your brother," she said, pulling back to make eye contact with him.

He smiled at the thought, he knew she wouldn't do that to him, to them. The true satisfaction was knowing his brother never would be with her. His dream was coming true at last. No one could stop them from being together now, not even Christian or Phillip Manelli.

They could and would deal with that later. First things were first, though.

He kissed her again, loving how she melted against him. But then she abruptly pulled back.

"Later," she murmured. "After we get our baby back. Then I'll make hot, mad, passionate love to you over and over."

"I want that too, more than you could begin to imagine." Too bad they didn't have time to stop at a hotel on Mr. Manelli's expense. But they were on a strict schedule and were already wasting time. They had to go get their baby, bring him home.

"What are we waiting for?" Lissa suddenly snapped.

The hotel room, Pete thought.

"We're wasting precious time," she said. He was amazed at her swift mood shift. "Let's go get our baby, and then go home and start our lives together."

Go home, he mused. *Yes, excellent idea.*

As he took off like a shot, she asked him, "Is the baby a boy or a girl?"

Boy or girl?

Lissa eyed the silver Honda Civic in the driveway at the cabin as they drove up. Christian's car. How had he get there so quickly? On second thought, had that really been him at his apartment? She hadn't seen his face, but the man she'd seen on the balcony had the same build as Christian, and he had been wearing the same clothes as he'd had on earlier, and that had been his voice calling after her. It definitely had been him at his apartment.

Did he know a shortcut? Had he passed them without her noticing? Had Pete driven too slowly? She didn't think so. He'd exceeded the speed limit the whole way there.

It didn't matter if Christian was there, she told herself. She was with Pete now. They were going to get their baby and then spend their future together.

I love you, Lyn, a voice said in her head.

Just stay the hell away from me, the same voice went on. *Never come near me again.*

Ana Lissa.

Leigh.

"Stop," she yelled frantically. She bent down, holding her head in her hands as though she was trying to soothe a headache.

"What is it?" Pete asked. He sounded panicked. "Are you okay?"

"Voices in my head."

"What voices?"

She was about to answer him when she jolted her head up and stared at the front door of the cabin. Christian was there talking to a woman at the door.

"Bastard," she hissed. She wanted to scratch his face with her fingernails, hopefully scarring him for life.

I always knew it was you.

Mommy loves you, lil' one. You'll be here with me soon. Won't be long now and then we'll go find Daddy.

The same voice again. She could picture herself rubbing her stomach.

Christian turned around and looked straight at her. She couldn't tell what he was thinking, but he seemed nervous. She wondered why. *It's over for you,* she promised silently, *you and your cockamamie attitude.*

Daddy's always right.

Christian turned away from Lissa as the door of the cabin opened.

"Oh, Lynley," the young woman who'd opened the door said. "Come and see our daughter. She's beautiful but we still haven't named her."

Daughter? He couldn't have been wrong about the baby being a boy. "Bessie," he began. She touched his shoulder and tried to kiss him. He backed away.

"Bessie, you have my and Lissa's son. Go get him and give him to me now."

"Son?" She was baffled by his words. "We don't have a son."

She looked past Christian. He turned and saw Lissa and Pete heading toward the cabin.

You bitch, Bessie, the voice in Lissa's head said.

Bessie stared from Pete to Christian and back again. *Two Lynleys? Impossible?*

Christian grabbed her as she started to collapse on him.

85

CHAPTER THIRTEEN

As Bessie came to, Pete laid a hand on Lissa's shoulder to comfort her.

She jerked away. "Don't touch me, you bastard," she said. "Don't ever touch me."

Where'd that come from? Pete wondered. *Was she starting to get her memory back?*

Christian watched with satisfaction, until Lissa turned on him.

"You've been lying to me," she exclaimed. "You kidnapped my baby."

It was Pete's turn to smile with satisfaction.

"I did not," Christian said. He pointed a finger at his brother. "It was him and your father."

"The only baby that's here," Bessie said, "is my baby. Mine and Lynley's." But she looked from Pete to Christian, as if uncertain which Lynley was the father.

"Bessie, give us the baby," Pete said, moving toward her in hopes of assuring her that it was okay. "We'll give her back."

Her? Lissa thought. How did he know it was a girl unless he'd seen her? Could she have been wrong about Pete's involvement in the kidnapping of her baby, and Christian be right? Doubts filled her brain. Or was Pete trying to trick Bessie?

"Pete," she said, "did you see the baby before you picked me up?"

"No. I just knew this is where our baby was. I'd received some tips from some people I know."

"I see." Or did she?

While the others were looking at Lissa, Bessie ran back into the cabin. She slammed the door shut and bolted it. A few seconds later, they heard loud noises from inside in the cabin, as if she was moving furniture to barricade the door.

Over all of that noise, they could hear the incessant crying of a baby inside the cabin. They had to figure out a way inside.

Lissa pounded on the door. "Give me my baby, bitch." She turned to the men. "What now?" she screamed. She looked around for something to smash the window, but she didn't know where the baby was and didn't want to harm him.

"Isn't there a backdoor?" Christian asked.

You would know, Lissa thought bitterly.

Christian took off around the back, with Pete and Lissa running after him. When they reached the back door, Bessie was there, holding the baby. She had something else in her hand, but Lissa couldn't tell what it was.

"Stay away from us or I'll kill you all," Bessie said. She was obviously distraught.

The baby was screaming, a pained cry for comfort and food. The sound of his cries were agony for Lissa, and she wanted nothing more than to grab her baby from Bessie, She almost did, except that Bessie revealed what was hidden in her hand. A gun, pointed right at Lissa.

"This is my baby and no one is getting their hands on her."

"Give her to us," Christian said in a stern voice.

Her, Lissa thought. *There it was again. So, Christian was lying about that too, huh? What else was he lying about?*

The three of them stood gaping at Bessie, not knowing what to do next. They couldn't take the chance that the gun was loaded.

You will be with Mommy soon, the voice in Lissa's voice chanted.

She tried to get a better look at the baby, to see his or her face, but Bessie saw what Lissa was trying to do. She turned the baby away and kept the gun aimed at Lissa.

"Back away, bitch," Bessie ordered. "I will kill you. I swear to God, I'll kill you, I will kill all of you."

Pete stared at Bessie, unsure what to do. She was sounding like a real killer, but he knew she wouldn't hurt a fly This wasn't the Bessie he knew, but she felt threatened because they were trying to take her baby away. She had no clue that the baby wasn't hers. It wasn't even a girl. That was how sick she was.

Lissa daringly took one step closer to Bessie and the baby. Christian tried to hold her back, but she fought him off. Bessie screamed out a warning and pulled the trigger. Christian pulled Lissa down to the ground and threw himself on top of her. He was more concerned about her life than his own. Their son needed his mother more than he needed his father.

The gun barely made a sound as it fired. The bullet hit a tree and ricocheted back, hitting Pete in the head. Christian stared at his brother in astonishment as Pete just stood there blinking. The bullet had fallen to the ground near Christian. He got up to examine it. It was a gumball. The gun was a toy.

Bessie started sobbing uncontrollably and sat down on the ground, the still wailing baby sprawled on her lap. Christian ran over and took the baby. Bessie didn't resist, and he carried the baby to Lissa and placed him in her arms.

He took a good look at the baby and knew in seconds who the father was. The boy was the splitting image of his father.

"Thank you," she sobbed. She didn't know how she'd ever repay him. Looking down at the baby, she saw that he looked exactly like Christian. She smiled at that and bent down to kiss her son, then brushed away the wet spots her tears left on his cheeks.

The baby stopped crying the second Christian laid him in her arms. It was as though he knew he was finally in his mother's arms; he was home. He lifted his arms up to her face as though to grab hold of her, to make sure it was really her. She grasped one of his hands and kissed his tiny fingers.

"My son, our son," she cried to Christian.

He smiled and kissed both of them on the tops of their heads.

"Give me my baby back," Bessie screamed.

I always knew it was you, Lissa mouthed to Christian, before he went to attend to Bessie and his brother, who was rubbing his sore head.

Phillip and Cassie suddenly walked around the side of the cabin. "What the hell is going on here?" Phillip demanded.

"They kidnapped my baby," Bessie cried as she ran to her mother. "Give me back my baby." She sounded like a little kid whose mother had just taken away her favorite toy.

"Oh, Bessie," Cassie said, holding her daughter. "Where have you been? I've been looking for you for months."

"Mommy," Bessie wailed in her mother's arms. "My baby, my daughter," Bessie screamed again, shaking uncontrollably.

"Bessie, listen to me." Cassie held her daughter's face in her hands. "You had a miscarriage months ago." She had been at the hospital in Briarton with Bessie, had taken her there herself. Bessie had been devastated by the loss, and soon after she had been released from the hospital, she had disappeared. Cassie had assumed Pete had had something to do with her disappearance and had been worried sick about her ever since.

"No, no, no," Bessie yelled in denial. She looked at Pete. "Lynley, make her give me back our daughter."

Lissa looked from Pete to Christian. Pete was the father of Bessie's baby? This was getting more and more bizarre by the minute.

"I don't know what she's talking about," he mumbled.

"So, Pete," Lissa began slowly, contemplating how to play this out. "What makes you think we slept together and you fathered my son?" She hadn't yet regained her memory, but she was starting to figure things out.

Oh, no, Pete thought. He really had to work his magic here to convince her, make her believe that they had indeed made love, and he had fathered her son.

"On the night of your so-called anniversary," he answered, "with my so-called brother—"

"Go on," Christian said.

"Yes, go on. Tell them the truth, dear."

"They all turned at the sound of another voice. Pete and Christian's mother, Laurel, had arrived.

Pete kept his attention on Lissa. "You were tired and sleeping in the spare room. I came in and we made love. You practically begged me to make love to you, and you knew it was me and not Christian." He knew that for a fact. "When I heard you were pregnant, I knew the baby was mine." He had known otherwise when he'd first looked at the baby, but if he could get the woman, everything else would work its way out.

Lissa turned around and stared at Christian for a moment before speaking. "Right, I remember." She didn't really. "Christian and I were celebrating our anniversary in Whistler, and we conceived our son that night." At least that's what Christian had told her yesterday about the conception of their child.

Christian let out a sigh of relief.

Pete's mouth dropped open as he stared at her, wide eyed. "Then who did I sleep with?" He knew he'd slept with someone that night. It had to have been Lissa.

They all looked at each other and then at Bessie.

Bessie gazed up at Pete. "It was amazing, wonderful," she said dreamily. "And we created a daughter together. She's inside sleeping."

"Bessie, honey," Cassie said in a sweet and calm voice, "we already went through this." She tried to soothe her daughter. "Remember, you had a miscarriage."

Bessie sobbed in her mother's arms, and then she wrenched herself free and tried to cling to Pete. "No Lynley, tell her she's wrong."

"Uh-uh . . ." Realizing he'd be caught in his web of lies, he was speechless and had to think fast. He would not go to jail for this. He glanced around at his surroundings, thinking about what to do next. "Bessie stole the baby from the van and brought him here."

"So you knew where he was this whole time?" Lissa asked.

"Yes, but for good reason I didn't tell you I knew where he was until today. You see, it was Bessie's state of mind. I had to figure out how to get the baby away from her so we could have him back. She never let him out of her sight. I don't think she's slept since she took him. I've been keeping close watch on them to make sure he stayed safe until we could take him and start our lives, really start our lives."

"Uh-huh." Lissa wasn't buying it.

"I knew she came here, so I came here right away the first day, after I left your place."

Out of the corner of his eye he noticed Liam coming toward him. *Think fast, think fast.* In a split second he was running for the cliff with Liam racing after him, gun in hand.

"Pete, no!" his mother screamed. "We can work this out. There's a reasonable explanation."

Seconds later he jumped off the cliff, flying toward the rough and rocky ocean below.

"Pete!" Laurel shrieked. "Not my baby, come back."

"He's gone, Mom," Christian said, placing his hands on her shoulders to comfort her.

"No!" Laurel screamed again. She fell to the ground on her hands and knees, sobbing uncontrollably and banging her fists on the ground.

Realizing he could do nothing for his mother, Christian joined Liam at the edge of the cliff. They couldn't see Pete's body on the rocks below or in the water. The only things they saw were trees, rocks, and the restless ocean.

CHAPTER FOURTEEN

When Lissa came out of the cabin after changing and feeding her son, she stared into the eyes of a unfamiliar but familiar face. Placing her free hand over her mouth, she gasped. "Oh my God."

Monica Manelli took her into her arms, tears running down her face, careful not to crush the baby. He'd been through enough in his short life.

Phillip's mouth gaped open. It was as though he had seen a ghost.

Monica turned to him. "What's the matter, Phillip? You look like you've seen a ghost." If she was going down, she was taking him with her.

"Monica." He tried to look pleased to see his ex-wife.

She walked over to him. "Bet you never expected to see me again, did you, Phillip?"

She pinched his cheek. He was speechless.

"But you know, Phillip," she went on, "I'm a survivor. Thought you knew that."

"I don't know what you're talking about, Monica."

"Stop with the lies," she said, her voice rising.

"What is she talking about, Phillip?" Cassie asked. She intrigued by Monica's sudden appearance and wondered where she'd been all these years.

"I don't know," he said.

Monica turned to her daughter. "Lissa, I need to tell you something very important."

"Monica!" Phillip's eyes grew wide as he clenched his fists at his sides. "You've been gone for years, abandoned your children."

"Where have you been all these years?" Cassie asked, and immediately got a *shut up* look from Phillip.

"Why don't you ask your husband?" Monica suggested.

Cassie glanced at Phillip and then at Monica. "Somebody please tell me what is going on," she yelled, even though she was the sort of woman who never yelled.

Phillip spoke before anyone else could. "She set her own house on fire and then took off, abandoning everyone, including her children, letting us all believe she was dead."

"No, that's not it," Monica said through clenched teeth. "You set my house on fire, you literally dragged me out of the burning house, drove me to Vancouver, and dumped me on the streets to die. You didn't expect me to survive one day, did you?" She jabbed a finger into his shoulder.

Cassie glared at her husband. "You did what?" She smacked him in the face as she yelled at him. A gut feeling told her Monica was telling the truth. Did she know her husband at all? Was there more? Why had he done this to his ex-wife, the mother of his children?

Lissa felt like she'd been hit by a tornado. The baby continued to sleep comfortably in her arms. He was as content as could be, not a care in the world. She wished she felt the same. What did her mother have to tell her? She wanted to butt in and ask but it didn't look like a convenient time, what with Cassie punching her husband and yelling, "attempted murder."

Monica turned to Lissa and let out a long, shallow sigh. "Lissa . . . I love you."

"I love you too." Her mother had never been mushy. Had her years on the street changed her that much?.

"I'm not your mother. Not your biological mother anyways."

Nobody moved or said a word.

Lissa looked at all the people there. Was her mother among the group? The only possibilities were . . .

Monica went on. "Cassie is."

Lissa stared in wonder at her father's wife. Cassie has lost a baby. She was that baby?

"What?" Cassie screamed. "You bastard." She started pummeling Phillip again. He just stood there and took it, as if he knew he'd deserved it.

Lissa walked over to him. "You controlling bastard." All the doting, all the gifts . . .

"I'm sorry," he said, but Lissa could tell he wasn't sorry.

"Why? Why would you do this?" Lissa asked, tears running down her face. She was starting to shake. She looked around to see who could hold her son and handed him to Monica, so she could focus all her attention on her father.

"I did it to protect you," Phillip said. "You are the apple of my life, my whole reason for living."

"Liar." She didn't believe it.

"Cassie and I had an affair while I was married to Monica," he explained. "Cassie got pregnant. I knew she couldn't raise two babies on her own, so both babies—"

"Excuse me?" Cassie yelled.

It didn't matter anymore, he thought. *It was all over.* "Lissa was born first. Monica and I took her."

"My God." Cassie realized she didn't know her husband at all. "You took my baby from me?"

"Cassie, I'm sorry," he apologized and lowered his head. "Bessie stayed with you and we decided not to tell her I was her father."

"No you decided." Phillip decided everything, controlled everything.

Cassie felt the tears flood her face and fall.

""Monica knew of course," Phillip said.

"He made me do it," Monica said, defending herself. "You know how controlling he is. If I hadn't agreed, he probably would have gotten rid of both babies. So I faked my pregnancy when we found out Cassie was pregnant, and when Ana Lissa was born, she was brought to me and when the second baby came out you kept her." How could have she done such a horrific thing? But Phillip had coerced her into doing it.

"Good God." Cassie realized her husband really thought he could control the world and everyone in it.

"I'm so sorry, Lissa," Monica went on. "Your father made me do it. I had no choice. He just handed you to me." At the time, she couldn't think of any way around it. Phillip really had control over her. He controlled every step, every move she ever made, just as he now controlled his daughter, son, and current wife. "I didn't have any choice." Or had she?

Lissa didn't know what to say to Monica. She'd cost her a lifetime with her mother. Could she ever forgive her, even though she knew her father had instigated the whole thing?

"Which is why," Phillip said, "I had to take control when your son was born. You couldn't have him. You would've found out."

"So Christian was right," Lissa said. "You were involved in my son's kidnapping?"

"Did it ever occur to you," Christian said, "that Lissa probably never would've found out? But if you hadn't kidnapped our son, I never would've found Monica."

"You found Monica?" Phillip asked, shocked. He should have known. It was all Christian's fault.

"That's right. I went to the alley and found her. Lissa had a dream about her, and also saw her in the alley when we went there."

A flashback of the woman in Christian's bed swam through Lissa's head. She turned to Monica. "It was you in Christian's bed?"

"Yes, dear." Monica smiled at her. "You ran out too fast. We couldn't catch you."

Overwhelmed, Lissa went to Monica and hugged her. Then she walked over to Cassie and hugged her too. "I'm so sorry."

"Me too. I'm sorry too."

Liam arrested Phillip and put him in his car, and then arrested Monica. Lissa begged him not to take her, but he apologized and said he didn't have a choice. She was guilty of kidnapping, even though she had felt at the time that she didn't have a choice.

Like a flash of lightning, past memories started sweeping into Lissa's mind, more than she'd like to have.

CHAPTER FIFTEEN

They hadn't yet made love since finding their son. They were waiting until she was physically and emotionally ready and they had received the test results back even though they knew what that outcome would be.

Christian ran a hand through her hair and down her back. She found herself breathing more heavily at his every touch, more so than when they had made love in the past.

She felt hot suddenly and wondered if she had inadvertently turned up the heat again. It only took her a few seconds to realize it was a different kind of heat.

"Oh God!" She moaned in pleasure between kisses.

Christian slipped his hands underneath her shirt, and he found she wasn't wearing a bra. He was always pleased when she didn't wear a bra.

She didn't object to his caresses, so he continued exploring familiar territory. But not so familiar, he mused, since she had given birth; and he had to remind himself that they hadn't been this intimate with one another for almost seven months. Way too long for his liking.

Suddenly impatient, he pulled her shirt off and suckled the milk from her breasts while his hands roamed up and down her body as he pushed her down on the bed.

He had already stripped down to his jockeys and she was taking advantage of his near nakedness, avidly exploring his body.

"I want to make love to you so bad," he confessed, his heartbeat quickening with her bold caresses. "I want to be inside you so bad, show you what making love was to us."

Lissa smiled at him in the darkness. "I remember," she purred. Lying on top of him, she bent down to kiss him, this time deeper, more passionate.

Her pants and underwear came off next. She lay on top of him again, feeling their naked bodies together.

Christian entered her while she lay on him. In one swift movement, he had her on her back, him on top. Immediately they began moving together, pleasing each other, caressing, breathing heavily, and finally screaming out in pleasure.

After he emptied himself inside her, Christian lay still, not wanting to leave her body, ever. They kissed repeatedly, not being able to get enough of each other.

"Wow!" Lissa exclaimed.

Christian reciprocated her words and feelings.

She ran a hand over his face and kissed him, "I always knew it was you. I love you, Lyn."

"I love you Leigh."

Lissa stared into space while she nursed her son. Her face was tear stained.

The blood and DNA tests had finally come back, it had been a long and endless wait. They confirmed what she and Christian already knew, they were the child's parents.

Lissa stirred on the couch as though he'd woken her up when he had come home. She became aware of her surroundings and his presence. She smiled at him.

"Sorry," Christian said, apologizing for disturbing her.

She smiled at him and handed him their son. He took him gladly, kissing his cheek and then putting him on his shoulder to burp him.

Christian glanced over at the coffee table and the live birth form that lay on top of it. He saw that he was listed as the father and she had named their son Jacob Christian Lynley.

"Nice name." He approved of it and the fact that she had given him his surname rather than her own. But he planned to change her surname to his before much longer. Now wouldn't be too soon.

It wasn't the most ideal or romantic place, but he knelt beside her after placing Jacob in his cradle and pulled out a small black box. "I love you, Leigh."

"I love you, Lyn." It was barely a whisper.

"Will you marry me?"

She sighed and made no movement, which worried him.

A single tear leaked from her eye, and she nodded as she whispered, "Yes." She pulled him to her for an electrifying kiss and a hug.

Oh thank God. There is a God. He smiled and kissed her again.

EPILOGUE

Phillip was imprisoned and given a life sentence. Monica was given a suspended sentence due to her time spent on the streets and a plea bargain to imprison her ex-husband. They searched for Pete's body for a week and came up empty-handed.

Bessie was put into a mental institution. Although the DNA tests proved Bessie wasn't her biological daughter, Cassie was heartbroken but she still visited her every day. She was still her daughter;she had raised Bessie and had loved her every day of her life.

Lissa had regained all of her memory by the time she and Christian returned from their three-week honeymoon in Hawaii.

As they walked away hand in hand from the cabin, a figure watched them from afar. He was not smiling.